The Journey Home

The Journey Home

Olaf Olafsson

ff

faber and faber

Many thanks to Victoria Cribb
for her invaluable assistance when writing this book.

Originally published in Iceland as *Sloo fiorildanna*
by Vaka-Helgafell hf, Reykjavik, in 1999
First published in the United States in 2000
by Pantheon Books, a division of Random House Inc., New York

First published in the United Kingdom in 2001
by Faber and Faber Limited
3 Queen Square, London WC1N 3AU

Printed in England by Clays Ltd, St Ives plc

A CIP record for this book is available from the British Library.

ISBN 0-571-20474-0

10 9 8 7 6 5 4 3 2 1

I'm getting ready to leave.

The fire is crackling with a familiar sound in the hearth and the aroma of last night's baked apples still lingers down here in the kitchen. The sky is awakening; I can just make out a pink glow in the east. It's as if my dog has sensed that I'm about to go. Instead of lying by the fire with eyes closed as she usually does early in the morning, she's trailing me around, rubbing herself against my legs. All is silent in the house; I'm the only one up, having slept badly as I've always done when I've been about to make this journey. But this time I am going to do it. Whatever happens, I am not going to let myself have a change of heart now.

I open the window to let in the morning breeze and take a deep breath. A bird perches on a branch outside the window, a blackbird, not unlike an Icelandic redwing, gazing at me with a slightly sad eye. A mist lies over the fields and the dew-laden grasses stir gently in the wind. It has been a hard winter but now spring has arrived and a pleasant sulfurous smell rises from the wood where the leaf mold has started to rot. The trees have turned green at last, their branches losing that gray look, and the breeze picks up the hesitant chuckling of the brook, carrying it over like a postman with good news in his bag.

When I awoke I saw two horses down by the brook. It was three o'clock in the morning. Without turning on the light, I wrapped myself in a warm blanket and watched them through the window. They moved slowly, blue in the bright moonlight. Suddenly one of them seemed to take fright. It bolted away over the fields, disappearing from sight behind Old Marshall's cottage, as if into thin air. I glanced back toward the brook but the other horse had vanished as well. This filled me with misgiving, though there was really no reason why it should, and I went downstairs to the kitchen to be comforted by the lingering aroma of last night's supper. I knew no better way of clearing my mind.

I blow on the embers in the hearth, then put on two good-sized, dry logs. The fire soon warms the room, reviving the scent of last night's supper like an unexpected memory. I wait for my nose to wake up too, wanting to recapture the aroma of the trout which I'd fried with a sprinkling of ground almonds, and the rich, tender wild mushrooms. And the apples which I love to bake after they have soaked in port for a long, quiet afternoon. My dog rubs up against me, whining unconvincingly in the hope that I'll scratch her behind her ears, and laying her head in my lap when I sit down in front of the fire. It is beginning to grow light outside, a pale blue-gray gleam illuminating the mist in the fields.

I sit a little longer, trying to summon the remembered aroma of the mushrooms and trout, but can't, no matter how hard I try. The apples won't let them through. "Strange," I whisper to myself, but I know better. Lately they seem to have been haunting my memory, the bowl of apples which greeted me when I arrived for the first time at the house in Fjolugata.

And to think I believed I had actively begun to forget those days.

I grind coffee beans in my old mill and turn on the ring under the kettle before going up to get dressed. My dog follows me upstairs. "Tina," I say, "dear old lady. You'll keep an eye on everything while I'm gone, won't you?"

Anthony is up and about. I can hear him in the shared bathroom which divides our bedrooms. I feel he has aged a bit this winter but his expression is still as open and candid as ever. I thank providence that our paths should have crossed. I don't know what would have happened otherwise.

My mood lightens at the sound of his humming as he rinses out his shaving brush in the sink. "De-de-de-de-de-dum-dum."

I was awakened before dawn as so often before by the ringing of a telephone. I sat bolt upright in bed, waiting to hear the sound again but was aware of nothing but the echo of the dream in my head. I have become used to this annoyance but it never fails to upset me.

The suitcases are waiting down in the entrance hall; I pause on my way upstairs as they catch my eye. Handsome, leather cases, given to Anthony by his father before the war. They must have been in the family for decades, accompanying them to Africa and America. And India too, of course. Strongly made, yet soft to the touch.

I glance out of the bedroom window. The sun has risen and its rays are stroking the mist from the fields, gently as a mother caressing her child's cheek. This time I will do it. This time I won't have a change of heart.

It's always been my habit to hang a mirror in my kitchen. Sometimes these mirrors have been nothing special, with spotted glass and frame coming unstuck, but they invariably come in handy when guests turn up unexpectedly. A quick glance in the glass, wiping off the condensation if necessary, to make absolutely sure that I haven't got gravy on the tip of my nose or flour in my hair, then I can greet my guests with a confident smile. The trick is to have a small shelf under the mirror where you can keep lipstick and a powder compact.

It was at the house in Fjolugata that I first came across a mirror in a kitchen, though I had completely forgotten the fact until the other day. The mistress of the house must have had it put up. Anyway, I immediately noticed it hanging beside the cooker the first time I set foot in the kitchen. It was a small mirror, hardly more than eight inches in diameter, with a beautiful frame: blue with hand-painted flowers of white, green and red. The mirror in the kitchen here at Ditton Hall is a larger affair and the frame is not blue but of dark mahogany. I found it down in the cellar the first time Anthony and I explored the house together.

For some reason, these two mirrors have shown a tendency to merge recently. When it happens it's as if I am whisked away and suddenly stand face-to-face with myself as I was more than twenty years ago, a young girl wearing a scarf over my fair hair to prevent the smell of food getting into it. I can even hear the mistress of the house upstairs and smell cigar smoke from the study. Sense his presence and begin to tremble for no reason. I don't know how long this lasts but I'm always confused when I come to myself, with an odd look in my eyes. As if I had been delirious. And I can still sense him standing behind me.

Marshall came trudging up the path toward the kitchen door, pausing by the brook to look down. The bridge was obscured by mist and Anthony and I stood by the window watching it hide the old man from view until he moved on again.

"He wants to get started on his spring chores," commented Anthony. "Look, now he's turning back to examine the handrail again. He's noticed a patch of flaking paint or a loose plank or something."

I was lost in thought, so we remained standing there in silence for a while, looking out at the fields, the brook and Old Marshall on the bridge, and I suddenly felt so unsteady that I had to grip the windowsill and sit down.

"Do you really think it makes any sense for me to leave right now?" I asked eventually. "With all the spring chores to do and the first guests arriving in under a month."

He patted me on the shoulder, then stooped to kiss me on the forehead.

"You're going now."

I handed Marshall a cup of tea as he came in.

"The rail on the bridge needs painting," he said. "No point in putting it off."

We looked outside. With the mist concealing any bald patches and loose planks, there appeared to be nothing wrong with the bridge. Nothing at all.

When I told Anthony the verdict last autumn he walked a little aside.

I sat down in the conservatory, wrapped myself in a blanket and looked out at the mist over the fields. Outside the glass a drip fell from the fading creeper. I was grateful to him for not breaking down in front of me.

I took his hand when he came in and asked him to sit down beside me. Just as he seemed on the point of saying something, we both caught sight of a butterfly fluttering from flower to flower in the conservatory. Its movements were slow but carefree, as if it was unaware of the autumn outside or had decided to ignore it.

"I thought they had all gone," said Anthony.

"Not this one," I replied.

"I used to miss them in the winter when I was a boy," he said. "Once I dreamt I could follow their trail."

The sun was low in the sky. We watched the butterfly in silence as it flitted from one sunbeam to the next. It was like watching candlelight reflected in a mirror as its silvery wings glittered in the late afternoon light.

Dr. Ellis's office hours are between two and four on Tuesdays. His waiting room contains five chairs, a table in one corner and a potted plant on the table. Above the plant hangs a reproduction of a sunset by Turner. Rather faded. I usually turn up at the appointed time on Tuesdays but sometimes Dr. Ellis kindly lets me come later in the day after dusk has fallen, which suits me better.

The first time we spoke, I said I hoped he looked after his patients better than the plant in the waiting room. Dr. Ellis is a serious man but I thought I glimpsed a hint of a smile. Since then he's had plenty of opportunities to be taken aback by my tendency to joke, especially the time he explained the results of my preliminary tests.

The waiting room windows face west and the view from them isn't much, though I wouldn't exactly call it an eyesore. Across the street there is a low, brick terrace with a barber's shop, newsagent and draper's at street level and flats on the upper two floors. Next to the barber's is a patch of wasteground where boys sometimes play football, and in the distance there is a railway line with little blue shelters on either side.

"Eighteen months," replied Dr. Ellis when I pressed him.
"Are you prepared to put that in writing?"
"Twelve to eighteen . . ."
"I'll take twelve."

At around noon an old train comes rattling along the tracks, puffing wearily as it draws to a stop between the two shelters. In the twilight there are no trains, but sometimes swallows flit around the brick houses on the other side, as noiseless as the souls of the departed.

Anthony rose to his feet during dinner last night, announcing that he wanted to say a few words. We'd just finished the mushrooms and the snails I had served with them for fun, but hadn't yet touched the trout. I was miles away, I can't remember where, when Anthony rose slowly to his feet and waited for me to notice, before clearing his throat and addressing us. We were sitting at the long table in the old dining room with the lights off and three large candlesticks on the table. I had laid it with a white, embroidered cloth and the blue-patterned plates which Anthony bought long ago in Paris. There aren't many left but there were enough for us last night.

There were eight of us: Anthony and I, Old Marshall, Miss Lynch who looks after the rooms, and the headwaiter, Sean Truelove. I'd also invited Mr. and Mrs. Wakefield from nearby Old Bridge Farm (they provide us with partridges, eggs, ham and cheese) and Old Marshall's daughter Lydia who lives in Bridgwater and is married to a doctor. They have a five-year-old son who comes to see us from time to time. I love having him keep me company in the kitchen. He always sits at the table in the corner between the cooker and the window where he can look out over the fields to the stables on the other side of the brook.

I slip him tidbits at every opportunity. He eats slowly and quietly and if he's in a good mood he'll sing a song with me. Then the sun will come out from behind the clouds and shine through the window, casting the boy's shadow onto the wall beside my mirror. Putting down my wooden spoon or ladle, I'll watch him for a while, quite forgetting myself, because all at once it's as if his shadow has acquired a life of its own and could belong to any small child. Lost in a reverie, I watch its slow, calm movements until he breaks in with: "Can I have some more bread?" or "Please, can you sing me another song?"

Anyway, as I was saying, Anthony rose to his feet and announced that he wanted to say a few words. It's been our habit ever since we first moved in together—if I can describe our relationship in those terms—to hold this dinner every spring just before we open the house to guests. We always invite the staff along with some of our neighbors, particularly those who help us out with provisions or with running the house.

There's no denying that in those first years it was sometimes difficult to put a good face on things during these evenings. Everyone knew that the hotel was only just breaking even, though I held my head up high and stuck to my guns. I have never been one to complain, but my hands are a constant reminder of the struggle during those years: they're not very feminine now, poor things. I also tried not to take to heart the locals' comments on the menu, which seemed exotic in those days of rationing and isolation. Some of them even made fun of the vegetables I took such pains to grow in our greenhouse, such was their ignorance. "Philistines," I said to Anthony; "I won't let them get me down."

Miss Halsey was with us for the first eleven years, but now Miss Lynch has been working here for six summers. Truelove has been with us from the very beginning and has really done us proud. And dear Old Marshall has been with Anthony's family ever since Anthony can remember and is devoted to him, more like a brother than a faithful servant.

As a rule we look forward to this evening with quiet anticipation, for whatever happens it marks the beginning of summer: bright days, open windows and white sheets flapping on the line by the laundry. The house springs to life like the grass outside; in the east wing, which has been shut up all winter, the staircase creaks again under the guests' feet, and the cooker is never cold from dawn to dusk. It's a long time since Anthony has been in such good spirits, though he does try to keep himself under control; fortunately he was taught as a child not to give way to unseemly displays of emotion but in the spring his childish joy tends to shine out as if through a thin veil.

"Spring is on the way," he began with a smile last night, "and I'm delighted to bring you the news that we're already fully booked for the first seven weeks!"

Mrs. Wakefield broke the ice by starting to clap. The others were quick to join in, as if they needed an outlet for their emotion.

He reminded them that we have increased the number of guest rooms from twenty-two to twenty-four by converting the sitting room in the east wing and the games room here in the main house, as these two rooms had hardly been used at all.

"I have a hunch—I know I shouldn't say it because it never pays to get one's expectations up too much," he continued, "but I suspect it won't be long before we have to start putting people on a waiting list."

He had become emotional and I thought I knew where

all this was leading, so I kept my head down, hoping he wouldn't make a meal of it. As usual he continued with a few words of praise for our dinner guests, first turning his attention to Miss Lynch and saying that everyone knew it was thanks to her that the rooms were so spotless and comfortable. He claimed to have firsthand knowledge of how much our guests looked forward to returning to their rooms at the end of a long day to be greeted by vases of flowers, birdsong from the open window and a soft quilt. (Though I think he went a bit over the top when he likened the quilt to whipped cream.)

Sean also received his share of the compliments.

"You make everyone feel as if they had done a good deed and deserved nothing but gratitude. You and your team are always ready to serve but never obtrusive, invisible but always at hand."

He said that Mr. and Mrs. Wakefield raised the best partridges he had ever tasted.

"And you have the welfare of our guests as close to your hearts as we do."

He contented himself with patting Old Marshall on the shoulder, then cleared his throat, groped in his pocket for a handkerchief and dried his eyes.

"My dear Disa," he said, lowering his voice, "you brought life and soul to this house at a time when it was cold and dark, and have allowed me to stay by your side all these years."

I got up and helped him to sit down—or rather thrust him into his chair.

"There, there," I said, "you'd better stop before everyone bursts into tears. Anyway, the trout's ready."

We sat down and he took my hand under the table, squeezing it every now and then, so I could tell he was still emotional. Dear man.

"Disa is going to Iceland tomorrow," he announced after a pause. "For the first time in twenty years. Let's all drink to her health."

They raised their glasses. Judging by the smell, the apples in the kitchen were just about ready.

In the thirty-second edition of the travel guide *A Gentle-man's Guide to Fine Hotels* the following review can be found on page 19:

> Ditton Hall is beautifully situated at the foot of the Mendip Hills, between Wells to the east and lush farm-ing country to the west. The premises are attractive with a relaxing atmosphere, while the grounds sur-rounding the three buildings, with their lily ponds and avenues of neatly trimmed hedges, cannot be faulted. It is very pleasant to sit on one of the stone seats imported from Spain in the middle of the last century, especially on a warm day when the birds are holding court in the garden. Inside, the hotel is peaceful and comfortable with nothing to disturb the guests but the worries they have brought with them, though even these should evaporate after a few days' stay in this place.
>
> The neighborhood offers facilities for fly-fishing and riding, while at the hotel itself there are two clay courts for tennis enthusiasts, and a cricket pitch.

The main body of the house dates from the early eighteenth century, and was bought in 1891 by Lord Lonsdale as a holiday home and hunting lodge. His heir converted it into a summer hotel and runs it with his wife. (This needs to be corrected in next year's edition; Anthony and I are certainly not married.) It is fair to say that the couple have been pioneers in this field.

There are twenty-two rooms (we need to correct this too), each one cozier than the last. The service is all one could wish for and every member of the staff is discreet and professional.

Yet there is one area in particular in which Ditton Hall stands head and shoulders above most other country-house hotels . . .

It's probably best to cut short the reference to *A Gentleman's Guide to Fine Hotels* at this point. Though I should like to point out, in case anyone comes across a copy, that the author has got it quite wrong when he says I serve quail with dates; it should actually be figs, which I have sent over by a friend in Provence. However, he's not the first person whose taste buds have been misled by this dish.

My reason for referring to this travel guide is not to draw attention to myself and the food we serve our guests but because I suspect we have this review to thank for the fact that it looks as if we'll be busy this summer. To be honest, I hadn't expected such high-flown praise after the guide's reviewers visited us last year. Not that their stay was less than satisfactory; everything went smoothly while it lasted. But there was an incident on their last day which caused Anthony a great deal of anxiety.

What happened was that Anthony and I were sitting with them in the summer house, where the old winter garden used to be, as we wanted to take tea with them before they left. It was an afternoon early in August, lovely and sunny outside with the pleasant sound of rackets hitting balls on the tennis courts. It must have been about four o'clock; at least I hadn't yet started to think about supper. We discussed cookery and I tried to put them right about some misunderstanding I thought I'd detected on the subject of goose and duck livers. They listened with interest and attention, especially the younger of the two. (They were both about forty, I suppose, but for some reason I felt one was a little younger than the other, though perhaps it was only the impression given by their different builds.) We got on well as they were both polite and good-mannered, though not very chatty. Anthony entertained them with stories about when he lived here as a boy with his grandfather, Lord Lonsdale, becoming quite animated as he was fond of the old man and can never recall those carefree, lazy days without getting nostalgic.

They were on the point of getting up to leave when I blurted out: "Isn't the name a bit of an anachronism?"

"I'm sorry?"

"A Gentleman's Guide to Fine Hotels. Isn't it a bit of an anachronism?"

They looked at each other.

"It's not only men who travel these days or decide where to go on holiday or for a rest cure," I continued rashly. "I can confidently claim that women have caught up with men in that area. We see it here. Don't we, Anthony?"

Embarrassed, Anthony coughed awkwardly and rose to his feet, muttering something about the guide being reliable and confidence-inspiring, whatever it was called.

He was saved, so to speak, by a young bird crashing into the glass in the summer house, creating a flurry as we all jumped up to help it. Our guests seemed relieved by the interruption.

The bird had recovered by the time they were ready to leave and was no doubt singing on a branch somewhere in the garden. I'd organized a picnic hamper for them, containing salmon, an omelette, some bread and even a bottle of rosé. But Anthony, upset and sure that my criticism would be the end of us, remained skulking in the summer house.

As I mentioned before, everyone awaited this day—or rather this evening—with polite anticipation, which always broke out into genuine cheerfulness as the meal progressed. But this evening there was something else in the air, something indefinable. Looking back, I suspect it was unleashed by Anthony's announcement that I was leaving the following morning.

When Anthony finally finished his speech, everyone began talking at once, Marshall telling anecdotes about Anthony when he was a boy, Miss Lynch and Truelove making plans for a staff outing to the seaside (though goodness knows when they'll have time to go), Anthony unable to resist recounting wartime heroics, which we'd all heard before and knew to be fictitious, and Mr. and Mrs. Wakefield making fun of our neighbor, the Earl of Helmsdale, who seems to live in the past and sometimes wakes them late at night by bursting drunkenly into the courtyard and trying to shoot clay pigeons in the dark. So the meal went on until I brought in the apple pie and Old Marshall's daughter suddenly caught my eye and said:

23

"How do you manage to cook such delicious food?" adding, "it's out of this world."

Everyone fell silent, as it was clear from her tone that she asked out of genuine curiosity, not an attempt at flattery. I didn't know what to do. If I answered her question it would be a tacit admission that I deserved the praise. On the other hand, it would be rude not to answer at all.

"When I first arrived in London in thirty-six," I began hesitantly, unsure where my answer was leading, "I lived next to Holland Park. My room was small, hardly more than a rabbit hutch. There was nothing in it but a bed, a washbasin, a wardrobe and a small desk. The window looked out over a little square with a bakery on one side and a chemist next to it. In the mornings I'd wake up to the clatter of carts outside or the racket from the kitchen downstairs where my patron Boulestin's friend Mrs. Brown lived. She was a tiny creature but a divine cook who taught me a great many useful things, blessed be her memory.

"Anyway, one evening, when we were sitting in her kitchen looking out over the square, where the light was gradually fading, I asked her what qualities good cooks should have. She answered straight off: 'They must be wicked sinners.' 'What?' I exclaimed. 'Yes,' she continued, 'they must be so wickedly sinful that their only hope of redemption is to bring happiness to others through good food.' "

I wasn't in the habit of referring to my years in London before the war, which perhaps explains why they listened with such attention. I don't think I've wasted much time thinking about them, either. I suppose I've probably done my best to forget them. But now with this story I'd stirred up the dust of old memories which would have been better left undisturbed. Perhaps my expression revealed my awkwardness, because a silence fell when everyone had finished laughing at the story of Mrs. Brown and her sins. Lydia, Old Marshall's daughter, restored the balance by saying:

"Sins can hardly be the explanation. Or we'd all cook far better than you."

Everyone burst out laughing again and we quickly raised our glasses. Then one story followed on from another about wickedly sinful people who couldn't even be trusted to boil an egg without disaster.

Seizing this chance to pop into the kitchen, I went out on to the steps to breathe in the evening air and the stillness which lay over everything. My darling Tina came to me and I told her I'd miss her while I was away.

When I realized I was well on the way to convincing myself that it would be best to postpone my trip to Iceland, I went back in to our guests, for I suspected this thought might take root if I were alone much longer.

His eyes change color in the dream, first brown, then blue, as his hands run over my body. His breathing is rapid and eager, his hair, damp with sweat, flopping against my face. I can't move; however hard I struggle I can't shift him.

I woke up early that morning. The repairman had been in to mend the cooker the previous evening and I had to make sure the gas was working properly again, burning with a steady blue flame. It was the middle of summer, the height of the season, and I couldn't risk the cooker breaking down or becoming temperamental. The repairman was still at work when I went up to bed, shortly after midnight, but when I came down at five in the morning he and his tools were gone. I remember noticing how neatly he had tidied up after himself.

I was quite satisfied with the flame and it was only when the clock struck two in the afternoon that I realized I'd been at it without a break since dawn. Not only had I wanted to keep an eye on the cooker myself following the repairs but there was also an unusual number of guests for lunch that

day. By two o'clock, however, the dining room had emptied
and the guests had gone out, some to cast a line for trout,
others to enjoy the mild afternoon by going for a walk or
drive. I looked around the empty dining room, listening to
the silence, and suddenly it dawned on me just how exhausted I was.

I've never been able to lie down during the day, never liked
wasting time in this way, so I decided to go and sit in my
favorite armchair in the games room in the east wing. I liked
this chair for two reasons. Firstly, it was extremely comfortable, not too hard or too soft, and secondly it looked out over
the hills to the north where beautiful cloud patterns often
formed in the sky.

I sighed with relief as I sat down and before I knew it was
so relaxed that my eyelids drooped. For some reason, my
rest was uneasy from the beginning. I quickly found myself
in that state between waking and sleeping where the sub-
conscious occasionally whispers that you're awake, yet at the
same time I was utterly exhausted, the handmaid of oblivion.
At first I thought I was in the kitchen of the house in Fjolugata. The morning paper lay on the table in front of me but
the heading was all wrong, with the date as large as a bold
headline: October 16, 1940. I was sitting on a high stool at the
kitchen table with the paper in front of me but the pages were
so heavy I couldn't turn them. Disconcerted, I tried to shift
them with both hands, but to no avail. It was then that I
heard the mistress calling from upstairs: "Disa, Christmas is
here! Light the candles! It's Christmas! Christmas is here!"

I stood up but hesitated when I smelled the cigar smoke
wafting to me from the study and heard my employer say
aloud: "She's taken her pills today."

"Christmas is here!" came the cry from upstairs again.
"Let's light the candles, it's so dark in here . . ."

I tried to walk to the door but my legs were as leaden as the pages of the newspaper. Then suddenly *his* voice intruded in the dream for the first time:

"Then Herr Himmler said to me . . ." Repeating with more emphasis: "Then Herr Himmler said to me . . ."

"To me, to me, to me," said the echoes in my head and I put my hands over my ears. Then the mistress's voice came again: "It's far too dark in here!"

Filled with trepidation, I closed my eyes as if escaping into myself. When I opened them again I was in pitch darkness, unable to see my hand in front of my face. As before, I couldn't move either hand or foot but now I was lying on my back and seemed to be in his bed down in the basement. He was lying on top of me, I could feel his breath on my face and his hands up my skirt. I tried to struggle but couldn't move, tried to scream but couldn't make a sound. When he entered me, I was jolted awake, trembling, in my chair in the games room.

I don't know if I was aware of my surroundings; all my attention was taken up by somebody crying out repeatedly. It was a terrible sound, like a woman in pain. She wasn't far off, perhaps in the next room. I leaped to my feet and fortunately found the key ring straightaway in my apron pocket. Dashing out into the corridor, I headed toward the sounds, which grew louder with every step, stuck my master key in the door of the room and burst in.

For various reasons I find it difficult to describe the next few minutes. All the same, I'm going to try to explain what I thought I saw, as briefly as possible, since there's no point in spinning out the story.

Her hands were tied to the bedstead but I couldn't see her face, which was hidden by the man thrashing away between her legs. He jerked her back and forth like a madman, his buttocks lathered with sweat, groaning horribly. Without waiting to see more I leapt forward, seizing him by the hair. We rolled off the bed, colliding with the bedside table and knocking a vase of flowers to the floor. Shrieking with terror, the woman freed herself from her bonds and, with even louder screams for help, grabbed a pillow and clutched it against herself. The man struggled dazed to his feet and when I finally saw his face I was brought up short. His expression showed neither violence nor anger, only astonishment and fear. It was then that I realized I had made a mistake.

I rushed out of the room, not stopping until I had reached my bedroom and locked the door. Oh, the embarrassment! The humiliation! At first I paced up and down, checking over and over again that the door was locked, then finally dropped into a chair in the corner and broke down.

In my headlong flight into hiding I seem to remember passing Miss Halsey somewhere in the main house. I also recall her asking, "What's going on?" but didn't answer. I suspect it was she who fetched Anthony, explaining that I was in a state about something. Anyway, he asked no questions when I finally let him in after he had waited a long time outside the door.

The guests I had burst in on turned out to be a couple from Germany on a holiday. They'd already spent two nights with us and had intended to stay for a third. Unsurprisingly, they decided to cut short their visit and left later that day. I took to my bed for the next forty-eight hours.

Anthony told me that he had refused to accept any payment from them, either for accommodation or food. I heard him out in silence and wasn't inclined to raise any objections.

When I woke up last night my thoughts turned to Mrs. Wakefield. Sean Truelove (poor boy being saddled with a surname like that!) had started talking about truth and lies. Why, I can't remember. He posed the following question: "If a sum of money is stolen from someone who didn't know he had it in the first place, has he really lost anything?" Continuing: "If someone tells another person a lie in order to save him from disappointment, has he done anything wrong?"

"For example?" asked Mr. Wakefield, who obviously believed Sean was getting a bit too philosophical for his own good.

"For example," he expanded, "if a man cheats on his wife (incidentally, isn't it strange the way men seem to think they have the monopoly on adultery?) but hides it from her, isn't he in fact doing her a favor, since the truth would only hurt her?"

This was an awkward moment, even for Sean himself once he realized how inappropriate his example had turned out to be.

Everyone—except Mrs. Wakefield, of course—knew about

her husband's infidelities. Anthony had once come across him having a bit of fun with one of the chambermaids who worked here for a couple of summers. If I remember correctly they were caught in the act in room 12. I could see the conversation was making Anthony uncomfortable; he stood up and opened the window to let out the cigar smoke, commenting on the weather, if I remember right, and pointing out the moon in the east. When I woke up last night I myself felt as if Truelove had somehow brought us all to the brink of a precipice in his stupidity, though not from any malicious intention.

There she sat smiling blithely beside her husband while Anthony pointed out the moon again and Sean tried to wriggle out of his own trap without giving away the truth.

"So, it's probably better not to know too much," I heard him stammer, and stored his comment away in my memory, as I can't deny that my life would have turned out differently had I left alone certain things I was not supposed to know.

Sometimes I can't help thinking there's a look of my father about Anthony. I noticed it yesterday evening when the girls had finished tidying up and Anthony sat on a stool by the kitchen fire with one cheek illuminated and the other in shadow. He appeared pensive and though he faced the window I didn't think he was looking at anything in particular; after all, it was dark outside. At that moment he reminded me of my father when he used to sit in the evenings at his desk in the dispensary that opened off his surgery, smoking his pipe and reading a paper or magazine, or whiling away the time by keeping a diary. When I couldn't get to sleep I used to creep down to him. I'd go into the surgery, and pushing the dispensary door a little ajar, poke my head through the gap and plead with my eyes to be allowed in.

"Disa, Disa dear. Are you still awake?" he'd ask, smiling. Then I'd run to him and climb on to his lap where he would pat my head as I snuggled up close.

"There, there, sweetheart, close your eyes and think of something nice," he'd say, and shortly afterward I'd be asleep.

They both have the same clear eyes and high brow, and a hint of sadness lurking in their smiles. When I was a child I thought it was weariness but now when I look back and picture him in his chair at the dispensary desk I think it was sadness. Of course, he was tired too; the life of a district doctor on the shores of the Arctic Ocean was one of endless drudgery. My sister Jorunn later said that he had watched too many people die without being able to do anything. Perhaps there was some truth in that.

Anthony seemed pensive. When he noticed that I had come into the kitchen he smiled at me and asked whether I'd like to take a stroll before bedtime.

"Maybe down to the brook? Just to get some fresh air."

We went outside. The sky was bright with stars and moonlight flooded the slope down to the brook, gleaming on the roof of the greenhouse at the bottom. We walked hand in hand and I thought he held my hand tighter than usual.

"Disa, dear," he said at last when we reached the bridge, "there's been something on my mind for the last few days."

We paused on the bridge to look down at the brook and then up the slope toward the house. The sight always reassures me.

"There's been something on my mind," he repeated, and at the same moment the moon went behind a cloud so that the only light came from a few windows up on the hill.

"I sometimes feel," he began, hesitantly, then continued, "I'm sometimes afraid you're not happy with me. I've sometimes been worried . . . well, because I am the way I am . . . I do wish it could be different but it can't be helped. I just wanted you to know how fond I am of you. I've never cared so much about anybody else."

I decided to put an end to this speech, as I knew what an

33

ordeal it was for him. Dear Anthony, how miserable he looked, as I could see when the moon appeared again from behind the clouds.

I tried to comfort him, telling him that I was as fond of him as he was of me. "I've never been happier than I am here," I said. "This is my home."

He hugged me. His cheeks were wet.

"You'll come back again, won't you?"

I couldn't help smiling at him.

"Of course, I'll come back. You of all people should know how often I've put off this trip."

A gust of wind blew across the fields as we walked back, swaying the grasses and shivering the leaves. We paused to listen to its whistling. It held the sound of spring.

"I'm going to come with you to Leith tomorrow," he announced.

"We'll see about that in the morning," I replied.

I was flabbergasted.

"Eleven pounds!" I exclaimed in disbelief. "Surely you haven't agreed to it?"

Anthony was as evasive as ever when the conversation turned to money, saying he considered eleven pounds a perfectly reasonable fee considering that it meant a forty-eight-hour journey for the driver, who would not only need to fill up with petrol but also pay for food and lodging for at least one night.

"Two, if he doesn't trust himself to drive back from Leith without a break."

However, I'd already done my sums and worked out—at a rough estimate—that petrol, accommodation at a clean bed-and-breakfast, and food and drink could not come to more than four pounds. I made allowance for his eating at decent places, though nowhere too expensive. That left seven pounds and I considered this quite enough, given that the depreciation on a four-year-old car would be insignificant over a forty-eight-hour period. Admittedly, it's a handsome vehicle: a Jaguar Deluxe, I remember Sean Truelove telling me. Of 1957 vintage, rather than 1958.

So I told Anthony that I found this amount outrageous and asked him to strike a new deal with the driver. I reminded him at the same time that this man often got to drive guests of ours who wanted a chauffeur-driven car; we always contacted him first, called him out and showed the guests into the car. In other words, he got all this free business from us without having to lift a finger.

"And what do we take for it?" I asked. "Nothing. Not a penny. We haven't even asked for a percentage."

Anthony sighed and put a piece of chocolate into his mouth, but I hadn't spoken my piece.

"And when we finally need him, he overcharges us! He doesn't scruple to fleece us!"

"Let's change the subject," said Anthony. "It's not good for you to talk about money."

I didn't like his tone and told him so. I also mentioned—but perhaps shouldn't have done—that it always ended up being me who had to sort out our finances; he should remember what a mess he'd been in when I came back in '41.

"Yet you could never be persuaded to sell a single painting and it took years of coaxing before you finally agreed to part with the estates in Devon. I feel ill when I think how much money you squandered before I got involved."

He stood up and went to the door. I could see that he was making heroic efforts to control his temper. In the doorway he turned back.

"He gave you a discount. A forty percent discount. Are you satisfied now?"

"What?"

"At first he wouldn't accept any fee at all but when I insisted on paying him, he refused to take any more than this.

Go down to reception and look at his list of rates if you don't believe me. It's on the desk."

When he went out, he had to restrain himself from slamming the door.

When I was passing through reception later that day, on some other errand, I took a quick look at the list of rates. I must admit that I felt quite upset with myself when I saw that the chauffeur appeared to have got the better of Anthony in their dealings, if you can put it like that, as it seemed to me after a brief glance that he had actually given us a more than 50 percent discount. To flare up like that, I said to myself, at Anthony of all people. It must be the trip.

Neither of us referred to the matter again, behaving as if nothing had happened when we were alone together later that evening.

But there is no denying that this incident has made me anxious and given me yet another reason to doubt whether any good will come of my journey to Iceland.

We're taking a break from our journey, after three hours' driving, to have a late lunch. I don't feel bad at all, having managed to doze off in the car for several minutes. The Jaguar is spacious and extremely well kept. The driver is pleasant too and doesn't bother me with unnecessary chit-chat. He told me when I woke up that I hadn't missed much, as nothing to speak of had happened while I was asleep except a brief shower, which was over almost before it had begun. Though there were still drops on the window when I opened my eyes.

There was nothing to disturb my peace as I sat in the back seat and made myself comfortable, nothing at all, which may explain why I began to wonder why I have always felt so con-tented on my travels through the English countryside. The answer probably lies in the words of the driver when he said that I hadn't missed anything while I dozed. Before I dropped off, fields stretched out as far as the eye could see, divided either by hedgerows and trees or attractive stone dry walls. The roads which wound through the countryside were in perfect harmony with it, as if they had been there from time immemorial, the work of God rather than man. Of course, this landscape is noble in its way, though I find it tranquil more than anything else and free from contrived exclamation marks. Although the scenery which passed before my eyes this morning could hardly be considered dramatic compared to the Icelandic landscape, it has the advantage of not distracting one's thoughts but resting them, allowing them to wander in peace. It occurred to me, as we drove past a mirrorlike lake, that from the time I first began to think for myself, I have tended to avoid journeys into the wilderness or anywhere that seemed remotely threatening.

As we drove past the beautiful lake, glassy in its calm, I began to think about the harsh Icelandic landscape, the cold mountains and the fields that spend more time under snow than in the sun, recalling without warning various trips I hoped I'd forgotten. Feeling suddenly unwell I asked the driver to stop and then walked down to the edge of the lake. Out on the water there were two men in a boat fishing. Their movements were slow—or perhaps it was just the distance that made it seem as if they were hardly moving at all. The air was clear and refreshing after the rain and I breathed in deeply, inhaling the scent of green growing things, and at that moment the clouds parted and sunshine spread out like a yellow cloth over the water and the boat. I felt better and we continued our journey.

"I can't remember ever having been carsick before," I said to the driver as he opened the rear door for me and asked how I was feeling. "I must be a bit tired still."

As I look out the window at the landscape, my thoughts can't help turning to the English people and their character.

The English—here I permit myself to generalize, though of course I'm referring mainly to the upper middle classes and people from old families—the English are restrained and even-tempered by nature. They avoid showing their feelings, and if they're at all given to self-analysis they keep the fact to themselves. They take care not to bother others with dissertations about their own affairs: after all, there are few things more tedious than people who bare their soul to one at every opportunity. Although my words may sound as if I find them cold or reserved, I don't mean that at all: many English people are warm and considerate and in every way comfortable to associate with.

To that point, I don't remember Anthony ever directly discussing the anxiety and problems his sexual orientation has caused him. Not once during the two decades since we first entered Ditton Hall together and he whispered to me, "Don't you think this could be turned into a first-rate hotel with a bit of work?"

"I don't think I could manage it," I remember saying.

"You? No one could manage it better than you."

"Oh, I don't know. Wouldn't it at least be sensible to wait till the war is over? No one will be coming here until then. And what with everything being rationed . . ."

"We'll have to make a start now if the house is ever to be ready," he replied. "The war will end. And one can't live on bread alone."

Twenty years and he has never complained to me about his lot in life, though some might have thought he had reason enough. The truth is often better left alone; there's no need to turn over every stone in your path, no point wasting your time in endlessly regretting something that could have turned out differently. No, it doesn't do anyone any good.

Sometimes you have to get a grip on yourself to keep your thoughts under control, but it's worth it. The reward is just around the next corner, whether it is a clutch of perfect eggs in a basket or the sound of birdsong on a still day. The soul can take delight in small things if one's dreams only leave it in peace long enough.

I got a bit chilled on the way here so I ordered hot soup as soon as I sat down. The girl was quick to serve me, as I'm the only customer. The other tables, twelve in all, are empty.

The edge of the village is marked by a small, smooth stream flowing between grassy banks. The sign on the other side reads Bevenford, while on this side a couple of dozen houses huddle along little-used streets. I doubt there are more than two hundred people living here, though the waitress said she didn't know when I asked her. Judging by her expression, she considered the number so small that she was embarrassed to admit it. It wouldn't surprise me; I remember when I had just arrived in Reykjavik either exaggerating or pleading ignorance when someone asked how many people lived in Kopasker, the north Iceland village where I grew up.

We drove slowly over the bridge into the village and stopped by the first building we came to, a green-and-white-painted garage with BP signs on either side of the frontage. I was feeling hungry but the driver said he wanted to check the oil and fill up with petrol, so we turned off the bumpy, unpaved road and drew up at the garage. As the driver had packed his own lunch, I left him with the car and set off on foot into the village in search of somewhere to eat. It wasn't far, quarter of a mile at most, and I got chilled on the way only because it started to rain. I quickened my pace, as my coat had been left behind on the back seat of the car and I knew I'd be soaked by this steady drizzle if I didn't get under cover quickly. I must have worked up considerable speed, judging by the way the baker and grocer stood and stared as I dashed into the high street.

The soup soon warmed me and I was pleasantly surprised by the delicious omelette which followed it. It immediately brought to mind a story about Madame Poulard who ran the Hôtel de la Tête d'Or in Normandy and was widely famed for the airy perfection of her omelettes. Someone once described them as being like ballerinas on water. So it was no wonder that travelers should beat a path to Mont-Saint-Michel simply in order to taste them, and it became something of a sport to try and guess what sorcery Madame used in their preparation. Some claimed she diluted the egg mixture with water, others insisted it wasn't water but cream, while others firmly believed the magic ingredient was chicken stock. It wasn't until 1932, after Madame Poulard had retired, that a countryman of hers called Robert Viel had the idea of sending her a letter to try to solve the riddle. Her answer was published in *La Table* magazine:

June 6, 1932

Dear Monsieur Viel,

Please find below the omelette recipe which you requested:

45

Break the eggs into a bowl, whisk them well, place a knob of butter in a frying pan, pour in the eggs and then shake the pan constantly while the eggs are cooking.

I do hope, Monsieur, that this recipe will come in useful.

Annette Poulard

The omelette was delicious and the glass of rosé I had with it warmed me to the core. Once Anthony had accepted the fact that he was to stay behind instead of accompanying me to the ship (the corners of his mouth turned down in sharp lines of protest before finally he nodded in resignation), he suggested I should keep a diary of my trip. He said it would be a good traveling companion for me, as it can be therapeutic to record one's thoughts or to exorcise them if they are disturbing. In actual fact, I've long been in the habit of writing down this and that but have never mentioned this to anyone, not even Anthony, so I was pleased to take up the challenge and accept his gift of a notebook. It was a good, thick volume with smooth pages, bound in leather.

As I finish my glass of rosé, I become aware that the weather is clearing up and all at once the sun has started to shine through the window where I sit, illuminating the room, the empty tables and chairs, the notebook itself and my hands, and the wallpaper, pale blue with white horses galloping over it. I'm feeling fine and the doubt which assailed me earlier this morning has now vanished, leaving me full of optimism about the trip. As I put down my knife and fork a little child on a tricycle pedals past the window for the second time, threading conscientiously between the puddles in the street. I resolve to remember him, and so draw a tricycle in the book with a little boy riding it and a woman sitting at a window, watching the boy. I sketch in her outline vaguely but take more trouble over the tulips in the flowerpot outside the window.

This morning I was reminded of my childhood in Kopasker when we drove past a farm and I saw two girls— sisters, I suppose—sitting in a meadow a short way from the road, playing with blades of grass. The elder can't have been more than ten, the younger perhaps two years her junior. My thoughts turned involuntarily to myself and my sister Jorunn when we were girls, as we often used to sit in the hayfield together making daisy chains. This morning I pushed this memory away, probably because I was feeling slightly carsick and so wasn't ready to dredge up the past. But now I welcome the memory, so I think I'll jot down a few episodes from my childhood. It seems appropriate to record them in Anthony's splendid notebook, especially since I have nothing else to do for the next half hour but sit here by the window and stare into space.

I ask the waitress to bring me a hunk of cheese and another glass of rosé. It's amazing how a simple omelette, a glass of wine and a ray of sunlight through a half-open window can raise the spirits in an instant.

Mother is expecting. I heard her telling Father it was nearly time as they sat in the living room this morning drinking coffee. I can tell by looking at her too; she moves in the same way as she did in the last few days before my brother Kari was born.

I'm the eldest at ten, my sister Jorunn is nine. We're best friends. And then there's Kari, of course, who's nearly four.

I would be lying if I said I was looking forward to having a new brother or sister, because I know I'll be stuck with looking after the child. Jorunn helps me as much as she can but I am the one whom Mother makes responsible.

"You're the eldest," she says, when I dare to raise my voice in protest. "We all have to do things we don't want to."

I used to look after Jorunn when she was younger and now I'm stuck with Kari. It isn't that I'm not fond of him, but it's so tiring having him tagging along wherever I go. Worse still, he's becoming a real nuisance. He kept hammering on our bedroom door yesterday when Jorunn and I were trying to talk, banging and screaming so loud that the maids could hear him all the way down in the basement: "I want my picture!" he kept screeching, "I want my picture." There's a picture of a railway train hanging above Jorunn's bed. "I want to come in and see my picture!"

I'm uneasy, anxious because Father has gone to visit a patient in the next village and I have the feeling that Mother is about to give birth. I watched him riding down the hill, his horses' hooves kicking up clouds of dust from the parched earth—it can't have rained for nearly three weeks. He has his own private route, which the horses know as well as he does, following the old riverbed to the end, then the track below the red hummocks until he disappears among them, heading for the sandy barrens to the east.

But this time it seems as if the earth has swallowed him up without warning and I'm filled with fear. I run after him, holding my hand over my eyes to shield them from the sun but it's too late. He's gone. I pause to catch my breath and try to imagine him smiling and talking to his horses or the clouds. I grow a little calmer with this thought and decide to turn back up the slope.

"What's the matter, Disa?" asks Jorunn when I suggest going down to the jetty with Kari.

"Nothing," I answer. "Let's go and see if we can spot any seals."

We dawdle past the Co-op, which is shut till three, past the old drying frames and fishing boats pulled up beside them. Dawdle, because I keep thinking I hear Mother calling. Each time it happens I stop dead and look over my shoulder. Then we carry on.

The jetty is deserted. Sometimes you'd think no one lived in this village but ghosts. We walk out to the end to look at the jellyfish and shoals of fry, then I sit down with Kari on a big rock on the shore while Joka (that's my sister's nickname) plays ducks and drakes. She's got the knack and I sit preoccupied, watching her and the sunbeams dancing from ripple to ripple out in the bay. Father will be home by six o'clock, if all goes well.

I'm supposed to fetch the cows home at five o'clock and make sure I get Kari back in good time. When I open the front door, one of the maids comes downstairs and tells me that Mother has gone to lie down. "It's just starting," she says.

She takes Jorunn and Kari into the kitchen, asking me to look in on Mother before setting off to fetch the cows. The other maid is up there with her. I climb the stairs reluctantly, longing more than anything else to run outside, away from the house, far, far away until it's all over.

At first Mother doesn't notice me standing silent and motionless in the doorway. I can see the suffering in her face and the sweat on her brow: she doubles up every now and then and the maid wipes her neck, chest and forehead. I know she'll start crying out soon. Suddenly she notices me and beckons. She smiles, but her smile is strange and stops short of her eyes. Giving me a kiss, she says, "Aren't you going to fetch the cows, dear?" Then hugs me, repeating over and over again, "My big girl, my big girl . . ." But her embrace becomes uncomfortably tight when the contractions rack her body and I hurry out as soon as she has released me.

The cows are in their usual place on the other side of the heathery ridge and give me a friendly greeting. I'm in no hurry to get home, and confide in them on the way back that I'm never going to have children. Never, ever. They nod in sympathy. As we make our slow way up the cattle trod, I see to my great relief that Father is home.

Joka, Kari and I eat in the kitchen with the maids but Father stays upstairs with Mother. I pick at my food, keeping an ear open for signs from upstairs but all is still quiet. After we've eaten, Kari goes to bed, while Jorunn and I go out into the cowshed with one of the maids. She asks me to pop back to the house to fetch a broom she's forgotten and just as I'm bending down to pick up the brush, the first cry reaches me from the window above my head.

The suffering in the cry is indescribable and I take to my heels. "Where are you going?" calls Jorunn after me, but gets no answer, and I can feel her eyes pursuing me until I disappear down the hill. Even then I can't stop but keep running as fast as my legs will carry me, over the old riverbed, skirting the edge of the marsh and the little stream, all the way to the spring under the crags. This is my refuge whenever I need to be alone.

Flinging myself flat on my face, I weep as if the world had ended, before finally getting hold of myself and rolling over onto my back, where I lie staring up at the evening sky and listening to the purling of the stream. The breeze ruffles the grass and the feel of it on my cheek gradually calms me down. I'm never going to have children. Never.

After a while the sky begins to sink toward me and I watch as it comes down to earth and covers me. A quick shudder runs through my body, followed by a sense of well-being.

I must have fallen asleep, as the next thing I remember is Father kissing me.

"I thought I'd find you here, Disa," he says, taking me in his arms. "You've got a little sister."

He sets off home with me. The sky is back in its place, the setting sun flushing and setting fire to a few fine-weather clouds. Yet suddenly it seems menacing. Trembling, I bury my face in Father's neck and burst into tears. "I don't want a sister," I cry, "I don't want her, I don't want to go home, I want to be left alone." I struggle in his arms, beating at him incessantly. He just hugs me closer without speaking. I go on and on until it's as if I'm delirious, feverish. I've lost control. I hear myself rambling on about an apple I had seen down on the shore that morning, a red apple I pretend I'd spotted in a cleft between two rocks but forgot to bring with me. I say I want to go and fetch the apple, I don't want to go home, I never want to go back again, I don't care about anything except the apple down on the shore, shining red between two black rocks. "I forgot the apple," I weep, "I forgot it . . ."

He gets me undressed and sits on the edge of my bed until I have dropped off. When I wake up next morning there is a shiny red glass apple on my bedside table.

In the relentless winter rain the world seems somehow diminished. The fields become sullen and gray, merging with the brook, until the bridge appears to serve no purpose, at least from a distance. I sometimes go for a walk on days like this to make sure that the brook is still in its place, its babbling unsilenced, for after a long wet spell my ears become dulled by the drumming of the rain.

Once I reach the bridge I can see the barn beside Old Marshall's cottage. There aren't many horses, we've only kept three for the last few seasons, but he's fond of them and I find their presence comforting. I sometimes go down there and think back to the days of the tuberculosis epidemic when Jorunn and I had to sleep out in the barn.

My sister Bjork was no more than a year old when she got tuberculosis. She came down with it first, Kari a week later. Jorunn and I both escaped and were made to sleep out in the barn so we wouldn't be infected. Kari gradually got better and made a full recovery in the end. I begged Father more than once to be allowed to sit with Bjork during her last days but he wouldn't be moved. I was upset for a long time afterward that I hadn't been allowed to see her before she died.

It was at the beginning of November. I don't remember the funeral, though I've been told that both Jorunn and I were there to see her off. But I do remember blaming myself for her death. "I don't want a sister," I had said to Father. That much I remembered from my delirium. "I don't want her."

As I approach, the horses turn their heads in my direction and watch me walking to the door of the barn. I think I can see the whites of their eyes ahead. I'm just about to open the door when I suddenly remember an important task awaiting my attention back in the kitchen. I turn round and hasten toward the bridge.

Over the years, there has been an ever-growing list of places of which I find myself saying, "I really must come back here one day." It might be a restaurant with a view of a harbor or a clearing in a wood, or perhaps a village up in the mountains or a white beach by the sea. "I really must come back here one day," I say to myself and may even scribble something in my notebook as a reminder. And yet, all things considered, the likelihood that I will ever be able to revisit old haunts grows less with every day that passes.

To avoid any misunderstanding, I'd like to make it clear that this fact does not weigh on me. But we've just passed a conservatory, which reminded me of a couple of greenhouses a short way from our cottage where Jakob used to buy me flowers. It seemed that whenever we took a stroll over the fields, we'd end up at these greenhouses, as if by chance, and Jakob would say, "Wait a minute," when he caught sight of them, and I would pretend not to know what he had in mind and he would pretend he believed that I had no idea he'd gone in to buy me a bunch of flowers. "Surprise!" he'd say as he presented me with the bouquet, and with an expression of wide-eyed astonishment, I would exclaim, "Oh!" before kissing him and flinging my arms around him.

I believe I've more or less stopped feeling sad at these memories of places from my past, as there's really no point in regretting the transitoriness of life. There's nothing one can do about it as far as I know, so I just concentrate on remembering the flowers Jakob used to give me, red tulips and white violets, his smile and his hands, sunburned and strong, yet so careful and gentle. I think about these things until the sense of loss begins to creep up on me and I have to take myself firmly in hand.

The cottage where Jakob and I lived is not far from Ditton Hall, half-an-hour's drive at most. But I have never seen any reason to go back there.

I think men fear death more than women do.

I'm not afraid of the end myself. Come what may, I'll know very little about it. After death there will be nothing waiting for me but a void. That is to say, I don't expect there to be anything on the other side, not even the equivalent of darkness, just nothingness, nothing at all. Of course, no one would be more delighted than me if the Almighty were to send me a brochure from heaven (I'm less interested in the alternative destination at this point), illustrated with beautiful pictures and detailed descriptions of the delights in store for us, the Chosen Ones. But as I've never received any such message, either by post or in a dream, I suppose I'll have to resign myself to the idea that death will be followed by Nothing.

A few weeks ago there was an outbreak of influenza here, the usual sort with a runny nose and cough, which sent a lot of people to bed. I escaped at first but Anthony was laid low. "Let me be laid low instead of him," I prayed to the Almighty, who is always forgetting to send me that brochure, because I wouldn't have minded a chance to lie in bed with a good book and a cup of tea while Anthony and the others fussed around me. But, of course, my prayers weren't answered any more than they had been the previous day.

So Anthony took to his bed and thought he was dying. The first day he was torn between the hope that this was just a twenty-four-hour bug and the fear that he had contracted a deadly disease. He took his temperature hourly and as the day went on and his fever continued to rise, the battle between hope and fear ended in a clear victory for the latter. I could read in his expression that he had already begun a mental inventory of all the things he would miss: the shy, fragile rays of sun entering the garden on a spring morning, a partridge served on a blue dish with figs and leeks, a glass of wine, a book. When I looked in on him that evening, I saw that he had been weeping.

It doesn't matter what Dr. Yardley says, Anthony thinks he knows better. "I can feel it in my bones," he tells me, "I'm going. This time there's no question. Disa," he says feebly. "You know I've made a will, don't you . . . ?" And I can't suppress a laugh as I sit on the edge of his bed, can't help myself, because it's hilarious to see him so sorry for himself. Once he's on the mend, his feelings are mixed. He is mentally exhausted by all the worrying but also rather sheepish, though naturally he's happy to have been restored to the land of the living.

Once, I did something I shouldn't have done. I don't know why; I'm not normally given to practical jokes and he didn't deserve it. But everything had gone wrong in the kitchen that day, the lamb I'd ordered was substandard and the vegetables I'd been waiting for turned out to be unusable. I was fed up with this endless drudgery and had asked myself many times that day what on earth I was doing trying to run a halfway decent restaurant in such a desert of taste and refinement. Anthony tried as ever to make things better by saying: "These things happen. You've been through this sort of thing before. Don't let it bother you, dear."

Unable to bear the kitchen a minute longer, I went upstairs to calm down. He followed to comfort me and decided to change his shirt while he was there. When he emerged bare-chested from our bathroom, I noticed that he looked concerned:

"There's a spot on my back," he said.

"The birthmark?" I asked.

"It seems bigger now. And the edges are not regular. Disa, can you please take a look. I hope . . ."

I had no patience for this. Instead of calming him down as I'm used to, I made an offhand remark:

"Maybe you're right."

This was not a nice thing to do. He hurried back into the bathroom and twisted and turned in front of the mirror in his attempts to get a glimpse of the spot which was actually nothing but a harmless birthmark.

"Do you think so?" he asked. "Do you really think it's changed?"

At that point I told him that it hadn't changed at all. He didn't believe me, thinking I was just trying to reassure him. But when I explained that I'd just been annoyed, he didn't know how to react. He was as confused as a child who discovers that its mother has played a trick on it. And can't understand why she did it. Can't understand.

I apologized. He smiled awkwardly. As we walked downstairs hand in hand, I could feel the vulnerability flowing from his palm.

My eyes begin involuntarily to follow the telegraph poles that line the road and then curve away to the west over the gently sloping pastures and low rolling hills, before finally vanishing into the distance. The Jaguar is comfortable. The driver has been telling me about his children, a son and a daughter. I close my eyes but can still see the poles. It is as if I am floating down a smooth-flowing river somewhere between sleeping and waking, then suddenly start up to find myself sitting beside my sister Joka in a bus bound for Reykjavik, the capital. We're on our way to enroll at the Commercial College and haven't stopped talking for a moment since we left Akureyri, the largest town in north Iceland. But now we lean back in our seats for a while and look out of the window.

On a low knoll ahead of us stand the ruins of a farmhouse. By the door sits an old man chewing a straw, while closer to the road sheep are grazing. They raise their heads one after another as we draw near, but the old man continues to stare out over the calm, autumn gray waters of the bay. To the left rise steep mountains, their scree-strewn slopes interspersed with patches of heather. They are haunted by elves and trolls, as are the glaciers beyond them. At the bottom of the bay, on the other hand, lie my forefathers, my grandfather and uncle who lost their lives shark-fishing in winter. Grandfather used to sell shark liver oil to the Danes and Mother would play with gold coins when she was a child. I've already begun to miss her.

The moor rises ahead and it's relaxing to watch the telegraph poles bounding past, though the jolting on these rough tracks is at times almost unbearable. When the road is at its best the poles remind me of a procession of people, straight-backed and solemn.

An old school friend of Father's, Vilhjalmur Borg, a lawyer at the Supreme Court, has arranged for us to have food and lodging at a guesthouse at Gardastraeti 9. It's run by a Danish woman called Mrs. Olsen.

I mean to study hard for the entrance exam and Father has coached us as well as he can. Although there's a year between us, Jorunn and I will both begin in the first year this autumn. Father and Mother have always sent us to school together. Of course, I wanted to go to the high school but Mother said it wasn't practical for girls. And that was that.

Jorunn has dropped off and her head is resting on my shoulder. I lean against her and close my eyes.

9 Gardast.
September 21, 1934

Dearest Mother,

The letter we wrote you yesterday went with the ship but time was so short that we didn't manage to send Kari's shoes. They cost 19.50 kronur. We couldn't find any we liked for less. Unfortunately, it looks as if there won't be any sales this autumn, of shoes or anything else. Joka and I played whist yesterday with Ella, who works as a maid for Mrs. Olsen, and Mina, Mrs. Olsen's cousin. Mina is tiny and very hard of hearing and always waits at table and makes a fuss of people while they're eating. When we'd finished our game, we all headed to Mrs. Hansen's——she's Mrs. Olsen's sister. She's a widow too and lives with her daughter. We really enjoyed our visit, but on the way home we got caught in a downpour.

Joka forgot to tell you in yesterday's letter who lives next door to us. A maid who works for the senior physician. She boards here with the couple's foster daughter. On the other side of us are two German women and a little boy. There are two dentists who take their meals here, two Danish men and a Danish girl, a German man and an Icelandic girl. Then there are two office girls, two seamstresses and another man, but I don't know what he does. Everyone agrees that we've been lucky to get all this for 100 kronur a month.

With love from,

Your daughter Disa

P.S. Mrs. Olsen is a really good cook. I've learned a lot from her already in these few weeks since we came south to Reykjavik. Last Sunday we roasted a rack of lamb in the oven. We made a good stock and put red-currant jelly in the sauce. It was absolutely delicious and Mrs. Olsen explained to me that the trick is not to leave the meat too long in the oven. When we took it out it was pink in the middle and melted in the mouth.

I know you've never approved of this hobby of mine but don't worry, it won't affect my bookkeeping, I promise. Even though it is boring . . . The meat tasted of heather.

I understand the *Gullfoss* is a splendid ship, the national pride and joy according to the shipping company literature which arrived recently in the post. I'm glad, as I don't have any other option, because I don't fly, that's for certain. Admittedly, I've sometimes mentioned lately that I'm not afraid of death. So it's a mystery to me why I should dislike flying so much.

The brochure I've received says that the *Gullfoss* is 330 feet long and 48 feet wide. There are three passenger classes accommodating 210 passengers in all, 104 in first class, 62 in second and 44 in third. The shipping company boasts of the ratio of crew members to passengers. There is apparently one crew member for every three passengers. Along with the steward and assistant steward the staff consists of seven chambermaids, nine waiters, two bartenders and two wine waiters, in addition to cooks and kitchen staff. The ship will call at Leith en route from Copenhagen, docking this evening and setting sail late tomorrow. The voyage to Iceland takes two and a half days but I get the impression things are arranged so that we have to spend three nights on board.

I mean to use the time well during the voyage. For one thing, I want to reread the letters I wrote to Mother and Father while I was at the Commercial College. Gunnar, Jorunn's husband, sent them to me after she died. He found them in an envelope in her bedside table. I also mean to carry on with this scribbling. I'd like to commit to paper some thoughts on cooking, as I've often been asked for recipes and advice but have seldom got round to putting anything on paper except notes as reminders to myself. I suppose it's because I've long resisted any tendency to use formulae or scientific precision in cookery. To me, the food itself is the best way of conveying what I have in mind each time; the feelings can't be adequately described in words. Moreover, I think there is a certain arrogance in precise recipes and I'm uncomfortable with laying down the law about how people should prepare their food.

The day before yesterday, for instance, I sneaked a few figs into the chicken I was to roast. I did it at the last moment because I had a sudden intuition that Anthony would appreciate the flavor of figs when he tasted the bird. Somehow I sensed it in his expression when he came trailing back from the tennis court. Sometimes I'm moved to cook snails in honey for the simple reason that I've seen bees buzzing in the sunshine; sometimes a bird singing on a branch will give me the idea of putting blackberries or currants in the sauce I'm preparing; sometimes the breeze billows the curtain over the little window in the corner and I think perhaps I'll serve baked cinnamon pears with the veal I have in my hands. Why? Did the breeze waft me the scent of spices from distant lands? Did it bring me a message from someone who was thinking kind thoughts about me?

How could I possibly put these feelings on paper without running the risk of spoiling the pleasure or revealing what should be discovered in peace.

Admittedly, there are people who can write sensibly about food and cookery. I had no sooner arrived in England than I began to read Eliza Acton and I still enjoy glancing at the articles Elizabeth David writes in the *Spectator*. She is almost never pretentious or overly sentimental and doesn't use words like *succulent* or *sizzling,* which I so despise. She seems to enjoy more freedom there than she did when she wrote for the *Sunday Times*. But as with everything else, this may just be my imagination.

Commercial College
October 28, 1934

Dear Father,

Winter descended without warning. All at once it began to snow. We were out in the park and I called, "Joka, it's starting to snow!" "Where?" asked Joka absentmindedly. "Look up at the sky," I said, "can't you see it's starting to snow?" We chased the snowflakes for a while, then dashed across the street and hurried home beside the lake. A little boy came toward us crying that he was frightened of the snow. He was all alone. "I'm scared of it," he said. "It comes from outer space."

We're having a good time here in town. Yesterday we bought coats with black sealskin collars. They cost nearly 100 kronur. The sealskin was the cheapest (17.00 kronur a coat) and also the prettiest. Mrs. Olsen and I cooked trout yesterday, fried whole, and lit candles on the table. Everyone praised the trout; I could tell by their expressions how much they liked it.

Mother has asked me twice now how I like the boys in my class. I suspect she's getting worried that I never go out. You can tell her that I find them a bit silly. Though Jorunn probably wouldn't agree.

68

I bumped into Vilhjalmur Borg in the street the day before yesterday. He was with a young woman I didn't recognize. He seemed rather drunk.

Do you think he might have a drink problem, Father? I don't think he noticed me, thank goodness.

I'm going to spend the night at Windermere where little Marilyn—or rather, Mrs. Marilyn Thomson as she should be called now—runs the Holbeck Ghyll country hotel with her husband. I wrote to her early in March, once it was obvious that I'd be making this trip, asking how things were going with her and hinting that I thought it was time we met up and renewed our friendship. It's now many years since our relationship cooled but I have tried to forgive her, though perhaps she didn't deserve it. She answered me by return of post, inviting me by all means to stay with her on my way to Leith. Although her letter was cautiously worded, I could detect the warmth behind it.

The shadows are lengthening and lie like fallen trees across the narrow road leading to Holbeck Ghyll. I won't mention a word about our quarrel when we meet, at least not unless she brings up the subject herself.

I've always called her "little Marilyn" because she was barely twenty when she first came to work for us, a slim, small-boned creature, less developed than girls of her age are usually. Her surname was Stevens, if I remember right. For the first month she worked as a chambermaid, helping out with the washing and gardening. These are back-breaking jobs and the other girls spent their time off amusing themselves, usually by shopping or going into town to have some fun, playing bingo or cards, or attending dances. But Marilyn showed little interest in joining them, becoming instead a frequent visitor to my kitchen whenever she was free from her chores. At first she was unobtrusive but kept a close eye on whatever was happening at the stove. Soon this extended to lending me a hand with this and that. Her help was appreciated, as she was good-natured and genuinely interested.

It is harder to find kitchen helpers than girls to do the cleaning (though I don't want to detract from the importance of their job) and after a few months little Marilyn was employed full time in my realm. I think it only right that those who cook should be well acquainted with other kitchen tasks, so she spent the first few weeks washing up and tidying. In the following weeks she graduated to helping me prepare the food, washing and chopping vegetables, cleaning the meat, ensuring that the jars were kept stocked with spices and things like that. Each chore, however unexciting it might have seemed to others, was performed by her with meticulous care.

She never complained about the work. I mention this particularly because there have been quite a number of girls who have given up after only a few weeks in my kitchen. Yet, I'm no tyrant, let me tell you. I have sometimes suggested they read *Down and Out in Paris and London* by George Orwell when their self-pity has started to get the better of them. I myself got used to the pressure early on. My patrons, Sivertsen and Boulestin, spared no one, but I never complained. No, I have never been one for that.

For six years little Marilyn was my right hand. I put myself out to teach her and couldn't have asked for a better pupil. Before I knew it I no longer needed to instruct her. She anticipated my thoughts, reached for a pot before I could even ask for it, removed a basil leaf from a slice of tomato when I thought it unpresentable and replaced it with another one, all without my needing to say a word. We worked as one and I can confidently claim that we felt comfortable in each other's presence.

But just when everything was going swimmingly the storm broke. It had long been my habit to greet the new day in the conservatory on the eastern side of the main house. The view over the meadows and the fields rolling off into the distance is lovely and I've even gotten used to seeing the two shacks on Helmsdale's property across the brook, with their gray corrugated roofs and half-open doors into darkness. I hadn't been sitting there for long that morning when Marilyn appeared in the doorway and took a seat beside me. It can't have been more than quarter past six. The light settled like a thin dusting of snow across the landscape and we sat in silence side by side, enjoying the peace. I poured a cup of tea for her. It was then that she dropped the bombshell: "I've decided to get married."

Naturally, I was completely dumbfounded by this news. It was all I could do not to drop my cup on the floor. I had never seen her with a man and hadn't thought it odd, since she seemed to stay at home when she wasn't in the kitchen. She read, went for walks, tended the plants in the greenhouse. But now her voice sounded odd in my ears. I couldn't bear the thought of losing her. In my agitation I blurted out, perhaps more harshly than I had intended: "You can't be serious? You're not pregnant, are you?"

She was stunned and speechless, and realizing it would probably be sensible to change my tone, I tried to do so, adding: "Who is the man?"

"William Thomson," she replied curtly—actually, I think it was: "*Mr.* William Thomson."

Well, well, my dear, I said to myself. Next you'll be calling him "sir." But I bit my tongue and merely asked what he did. She explained that he was a market gardener from Windermere in the Lake District who had earned a good reputation for his produce. Marilyn had read about him in an article by Elizabeth David in the *Spectator* and got in touch with him shortly afterward when we urgently needed green peppers and other vegetables following a mishap in my greenhouse. Apparently they got on well together on the phone and talked regularly after that, until little Marilyn eventually went up north to Cumbria to visit him. For some reason I had been under the impression that she was going to stay with relatives.

"Do you really think it's a good idea? Do you think it's sensible to marry a man you hardly know and move away to a place where you'll be a complete stranger?"

At that point she said she loved him.

I couldn't prevent myself from rolling my eyes at that and saying, "And you have a lot of experience in that field, do you?"

She stood up. Her eyes were bright with unshed tears and her voice broke when she said, "I thought you would understand me. Of all the people I know, I thought you were the one I'd always be able to rely on."

Then she turned on her heel and left.

"Marilyn!" I called after her. "Marilyn!" but she didn't look back.

The newly risen sun was beginning to warm the conservatory, but the tea was cold.

When she took her leave of us a month later, I asked Anthony to give her a necklace which I had inherited from my maternal grandmother. I was in bed with a cold at the time and couldn't bring myself to go down and see her off.

9 Gardast.
October 17, 1935

Dearest Mother,

We've been back at school for one and a half weeks now. Our new classroom is sunnier and warmer than last year. It's on the top floor and there's a view out of the window from where we sit. We're learning the same subjects as last year with the addition of commodities studies. It is unbelievably boring, but I don't want to burden you by saying any more about that or about bookkeeping.

I haven't told you yet that the first thing I saw when the ship docked was Nuna. She waved and yelled, "Disa, are you back?" And dashed over to me as soon as I came ashore.

"You've lost weight over the summer," she said. "You're almost unrecognizable."

Since then I've heard the same thing from several other people. This evening I'll be able to pick up the hat that's being altered. Joka went over to Hafnarfjordur to buy us slippers. Apparently, you can get really good shoes in Hafnarfjordur.

Anyway, I can't think of anything else at the moment. Do give my love to the girls.

Love from,

Your daughter Disa

P.S. It's true that I've started helping out in the kitchen at Hotel Borg. I completely forgot to tell you when I last wrote. I had a stroke of luck as Mrs. Olsen knows the chef, Mr. Sivertsen, who offered me work on Friday and Saturday evenings. I know I'm going to learn a lot from him. Last weekend fish soup and steak were on the menu. This Saturday there's a banquet for some Danish officials who are on a visit here in town. Sivertsen is going to cook goose for them, with ptarmigan broth for the starter. I can't wait.

You mustn't worry about this affecting my studies. Most of the other girls spend Friday and Saturday evenings at the cinema or skating.

I didn't sleep a wink the night after little Marilyn left. Around midnight a storm blew up and the branches of the ancient poplar rapped against the gable of the house while the rain lashed my window. The poplar had always given me the impression that it was kindly disposed toward me, often seeming to acknowledge me when I was out for a walk, as if it knew me. All kinds of birds perched in its boughs and one summer I remember there being as many as three nests at once. The community was surprisingly a harmonious one. But now as the tree beat relentlessly against the house, I was filled with unease, for it suddenly felt as if someone was in desperate need of my help.

There had been a coolness between Marilyn and me ever since our talk in the conservatory and as I lay awake I began to wonder whether I had been unjust to her. Had I reacted out of jealousy? I asked myself. Was I inconsiderate to her? Should I have congratulated her instead of trying to make her see that what she thought was love would only bring her unhappiness in the long run? I sat up in bed and asked myself again:

was there something else behind my words which I couldn't put my finger on?

I tried to keep calm but the noise of the storm frightened me and I thought I saw lightning flicker in the gap between the curtains. Shortly afterward I heard a distant clap of thunder. I resolved to think over the chain of events objectively as if I had been a bystander, uninvolved. I came to the same conclusion as before: that my reaction had above all been motivated by concern for her, though I couldn't hide the fact that I might also have been thinking of myself. She had been closer to me than almost anyone else, and I couldn't contemplate how I would manage without her. I had taken care of her as if she was my own daughter. Which is why I felt she had been so inconsiderate to spring such a decision on me out of the blue.

No, there was no doubt that she had let me down, and I made sure she was aware of the fact, deliberately saying to Sean Truelove in her hearing: "Some people think about no one but themselves."

Shortly afterward she offered to stay longer. I turned down her offer, saying I didn't want to cause her any further inconvenience.

All things considered, I believe I treated her honorably, though I might have been a bit sharp on a couple of occasions. I really do believe that it was with her welfare in mind that I reacted as I did. At least, I hope so.

So passed the night after her departure. Toward morning the wind dropped and at daybreak I put on my dressing gown and opened the window. I was exhausted but the breeze was too warm to refresh me. I went down to the kitchen and lit a cigarillo to calm my mind. The sunlight crept toward me across the floor and I walked to meet it, opening the door and stepping outside. A pleasant scent rose from the earth after the rain, and the grass had turned green overnight. A bird flew by with a caterpillar in its beak and vanished from sight behind the east wing.

I walked over to the poplar and leaned against it, my head still full of the night's preoccupations. As always, the tree's presence was soothing, but this time I felt as if there was something it wanted to say to me.

9 Gardast.
March 12, 1936

Dearest Mother,

I went back down to the telephone exchange yesterday, but gave up after an hour. They still hadn't got through to Kopasker.

As you can imagine, I haven't been able to think about anything else since our conversation. You mustn't think that I'm ungrateful to you and Father for having fixed me up with a job at the bank. I know it wasn't easy and don't doubt that many other girls would welcome the job. But after long thought and many sleepless nights I have come to the same decision as before.

It would do no one any favors if I turned my back on my existing plans to go abroad and learn more about cookery. Mr. Sivertsen said yesterday that he was sure I would get a place at either the Angleterre in Copenhagen or at his friend's restaurant in London. Just think, Mother: Copenhagen or London! I was so excited that I flung my arms round his neck and kissed him right on the cheek. He has been terribly kind and considerate to me. And he's expecting an answer very soon.

Don't be angry with me, Mother. Please don't, because you know how much I care about you and Father.

Love from,

Disa

Father looked exhausted. He was first down the gangway, stopping midway to peer around, but didn't see me even though I was standing no more than ten yards away from him, waving. He looked desperately tired, and didn't move on until the woman behind nudged him and whispered something in his ear.

"There you are, Disa dear," he said, relieved when I hurried over to him. "I couldn't see you anywhere."

Joka was at a typing class, and Father and I took a taxi to Gardastraeti so that we wouldn't have to be weighed down by his luggage. Just as we were setting off, a man came running after the car, gesticulating wildly to catch our attention. We stopped.

"The doctor forgot his bag," he said, panting. "I noticed it up on deck."

We thanked him and drove away. He was unusually plump for such a young man and when I looked round I saw him waddling back, dragging his feet.

"Your mother is worried about you," was the first thing Father said as we left the docks.

I was silent.

"Is there any use trying to make you come to your senses?"

I was speechless for once, not having expected him to come to the point so quickly. Finally I stammered miserably, "Oh, Father . . ."

It was then that he smiled with his eyes and said: "So you're determined to be a bohemian, my dear."

We didn't speak again during the car journey, and when we reached 9 Gardastraeti I helped the driver in with the bags. Father moved with slow deliberation and crawled straight into bed after greeting Mrs. Olsen and thanking her for looking after Jorunn and me.

When Joka and I came home from school that evening, he had gone to dinner with his friend Vilhjalmur and Thorunn, his wife. He'd asked Mrs. Olsen to give me an envelope. I opened it at once and read with Joka breathing down my neck:

Miss Bohemian, Asdis Jonsdottir,

You will find out one day how short life is and how little time we have. For this reason I am not going to try and dissuade you any further, I can see how pointless it would be. On the other hand, I do have three wishes to put to you:

Firstly, I would like to meet Mr. Sivertsen tomorrow, preferably between two and four. I mean to speak to him about the arrangements he has made for you in London. I wish to meet him in private.

Secondly, I would like you to do well in your exams this spring to please your mother. She deserves it.

Thirdly, I would like you to do your best in Sivertsen's kitchen on Saturday evening, as I have booked a table for two at Hotel Borg for eight o'clock. You can tell your sister Jorunn, who is no doubt standing beside you as you read this, that it would be my pleasure to invite her as my guest.

Father

Hands which were ignorant of what lay in store for them, eyes innocent of what they would see, afraid of nothing. An open smile and thick, coal-black hair, combed back. Of average height, I think, with broad shoulders.

I think.

When I try to picture him in my memory the first thing I see is the silhouette of his hands against white paper. He is sitting at the old desk which we bought in a moment of extravagance at an outdoor market that spring and installed by the window facing the garden. He's holding a pen. Dusk is falling. He turns to me when I bring him hot water for his tea. All I can see is the smile in his eyes.

"Jakob, it's getting dark," I say, lighting the lamp on the table beside him.

The twilight trickles in slowly and silently, wrapping itself around my feet, mantling our bed on the other side of the room. He shifts the pen between his fingers when I lean down and touch him. I see the shadow on the pages in front of me.

"Shall we walk down to the lake?"

Leaving the lamp on, we set off, walking hand in hand.

When we come down to the boats, which have been drawn up on the shore, I see a yellow gleam from the window up on the hill. I turn to him to point out the light but he has disappeared.

Darkness falls on the boats. I am still holding the shadow of his hand.

I must have been thinking about golden plovers and snipe when the waiter offered me coffee, which was why I responded to him more slowly than I would have liked. The food was adequate—bouillon, salmon and roast duckling— but I was amazed by the formality of the meal. The captain had invited me to take a seat by his side; it is clearly a much sought-after privilege to sit at his table.

About two hours before supper people had retired to their cabins. I went up on deck to get some fresh air. A young man whom I hadn't noticed when we sailed from Scotland came over and began to talk to me.

I gathered that he had just finished a doctorate in Old Icelandic literature and would be taking over from the professor in Copenhagen the following year. I didn't ask many questions, just nodded, as I wanted to be left in peace. But he chattered on, informing me uninvited that the passengers had mostly gone to have a rest, but would later wash from head to toe before donning their glad rags. He announced furthermore that the evening after sailing from Leith was particularly important as new guests had come on board who needed to be simultaneously summed up and impressed, as he put it. He talked as if he were above this sort of display, yet there was no doubt that it occupied his mind

"You'll be invited to sit at the captain's table," he said. "You're in the main suite. Everybody's been asking about you."

I noticed when I came on board that the passengers had a great deal of luggage with them, some even bringing iron-bound trunks. No doubt their clothes were carefully folded and wrapped in tissue paper. I imagined that all the little boxes I saw were for clothes brushes, sewing kits or cosmetics. Some of the gentlemen had *étuis* made of leather but none could compare with Anthony's. I couldn't help smiling when I thought of it. It contains metal holders for shaving soap, shaving brushes, hand soap, toothbrushes, toothpaste tubes and toothpowder containers. There are also many different types of pockets for razor and mirror, comb, hairbrush, nail pick and nail file, shoehorn, shoelaces, aftershave, face cream and scissors. Before each journey, Anthony checks that nothing is missing in this magnificent *étui*, making sure that the aftershave has not evaporated or the razor blade lost its bite. He caresses and polishes everything, and asks the busboys and porters to take great care of it when they are carrying it from the car to the train or up to his hotel room.

No, they couldn't even begin to compare with this, the little cases brought on board by the gentlemen. Goodness, what airs and graces they put on when they came in to dinner, looking so dapper and smart, their wives wearing the sort of distant expressions they had no doubt seen on Audrey Hepburn or Vivien Leigh at the cinema.

The duckling wasn't bad, but I was thinking of snipe and plover when the waiter offered me coffee. I thought I could hear the plover singing softly outside my bedroom window at Kopasker and see the snipe springing up from the marsh down by the road with its unnerving squawk.

"Kaffe?" asked the waiter, who was Danish.

I nodded and realized all of a sudden that it was too late to turn back.

The doctor of Old Icelandic talked nonstop. He said he was going to write a book about the voyages of the Vikings when the time was right.

"And the waves," he said. "The white-foaming waves and the sunbeams like splayed fingers."

I listened in silence, but couldn't see any white-foaming waves, as the sea had been like a mirror since we sailed from Leith, the breeze gentle on my cheek. The houses on land grew smaller, the gulls bid us farewell and the watery waste took over. Three nights. In three nights' time I would be there. And what was I going to say? What explanation was I going to give?

"I've discovered the identity of the author of *Egil's Saga,*" announced the doctor.

"Really?"

"I've been invited to give a lecture on the subject at the University of Iceland. I'll have to see whether I have time."

Why was I doing this? I put on my sunglasses, as the sky was now cloudless and the glare hurt my eyes. Why was I making this journey?

"Everyone's asking who you are," I heard the doctor say. "I said I didn't know. 'Never heard of her,' I said. You live in England, don't you?"

I made my excuses and went below. Nosiness. This Icelandic nosiness. Anthony should never have booked me into this suite. It only attracts attention. I know he meant well, but I do so want to be left alone.

"Who is she? Does she live in England? Asdis Jonsdottir— do you know her at all, boys? Have you ever heard of her?"

I locked the door behind me once I reached my cabin. I closed my eyes, yet was afraid to fall asleep as my picture had appeared to me twice in a dream the previous night. My cheek and arm were visible, but he wasn't there. When I woke up I had to wait for my heart to stop pounding before going into the bathroom to dry off the sweat.

"Who is she? Does she live in England?"

It was going to be a long journey.

I have brought along a few books, photographs and old letters which I mean to reread during the journey.

When I'd escaped from the doctor and reached the safe refuge of my cabin, I opened the little book that Father had given me the evening I sailed for England. *Help Yourself,* it is called, with the subtitle: *Advice for young people, illustrated with true examples and supported with arguments from the lives of good men.* Published in Reykjavik, 1892, compiled by Samuel Smiles and translated by Olafur Olafsson, the vicar of Guttormshagi. I remember this book lying on his table in the dispensary when I was a child. I suspect he used to turn to it for comfort sometimes when times were hard.

"Here, Disa," he added after saying good-bye. (I can still remember how tightly he hugged me and how long he held me.) "Here, Disa. Put this book in your pocket. It might come in useful."

He and Joka stood on the dock as the ship sailed out of the bay. He seemed so small, even before I went up the gangway. Sometimes, especially if I haven't had enough sleep, I have difficulty catching sight of him in my memory.

Little Marilyn and I sat up late and I must say, before going any further, that she hasn't lost any of her talent for cooking. The moment I took the first mouthful of lobster I knew I was in the presence of a soulmate.

"Nonsense," she said in embarrassment. "You taught me everything I know."

After the meal we stayed out on the veranda listening to the familiar evening sounds and treating ourselves to cheese and fruit—peaches, strawberries, apples and cherries—as companionably as if nothing had changed since we used to sit outside the conservatory at home at the end of a long day's work, talking about everything and nothing, or just enjoying the silence with no need for words.

The hotel is beautifully situated beside Lake Windermere, and although it is not built on high ground, there is nothing to disrupt the view to the south over the water and the Langdale Fells. As we approached earlier today, I noticed an oystercatcher on the shore and a tern diving for minnows. The house is neat and attractive, though not large, a former rectory, as I had guessed from the photographs. The annex where my driver is staying does nothing to detract from the view, as it has been freshly painted. It's a good thing he didn't have to pay for lodging at some bed-and-breakfast. Marilyn and her husband run the hotel and own it in partnership, from what I can gather, though naturally it wouldn't occur to me to inquire into their finances. The rooms are also cozy, proving that little Marilyn has a good memory.

In other words, I would recommend Holbeck Ghyll without hesitation to anyone who is visiting the Lake District in Cumbria.

During the last stages of the journey I had been slightly anxious about what I should say to her when I arrived, but these worries turned out to be unnecessary. They were both there to greet me as we came up the drive, and had clearly been waiting for me. Marilyn opened my door before the driver could get there, while her husband stood back. She had matured attractively, putting on a few pounds where they wouldn't go amiss and her smile and eyes contained the same sincerity, though they had gained assurance over the years. She hugged me and it was as if we had never quarreled. The porter took my bags and carried them inside, and once we had released each other her husband greeted me warmly and asked the driver to park the car behind the house and take some refreshment in the kitchen.

My room faced south. I ran a bath and lay in the tub looking out over the lake through the open window. A butterfly flew in and fluttered around me and I watched with pleasure as the sun shone on its paper-thin wings, turning them into a flickering spark of light. The sight filled me with a sense of well-being and I felt sure the evening would be delightful.

I had noticed how well husband and wife seemed to get on together, in a nice way, without artifice. My thoughts turned to them as I lay in the bath looking out at the lake and it occurred to me, as so often before, that my attitude to their marriage had been wrong. I pondered this for a while and was on the verge of feeling guilty once again, but told myself after further consideration that there was no point in brooding over something which was long since buried and forgotten. The main thing was that their marriage appeared happy. Satisfied that this conclusion was right, I dried myself in the breeze from the window.

After getting dressed, I took a better look around the room. It was spacious with pretty yellow wallpaper which seemed even more cheerful in the light of the afternoon sun. On the bedside table was a small lamp, a vase containing a reddish yellow rose, and a gardening book. On the coffee table lay brochures about the hotel and information about the neighboring district, as well as a silver cigar box, dried grasses and a cookery book which I had been persuaded to take part in writing several years before. No doubt I would have been better off not to have done so. During the evening little Marilyn told me that a copy was placed in every room in the house, including the downstairs drawing room. I asked her whether she was trying to frighten away the guests, many of whom had no doubt come a long way.

A vine climbed up the wall of the house by the veranda and although there were no grapes as yet, the foliage was pleasant to look at in the evening sun. We ate a leisurely meal and drank a refreshing, full-flavored Muscat. Mr. Thomson—or Bill as she calls him, thank goodness—stayed inside. Marilyn said he was mending riding tackle with a neighbor's groom. A shy girl, whom Marilyn said she was teaching to wait on tables, brought out the dishes, but left us alone otherwise. When she appeared with the fruit and cheese, Marilyn suddenly said to me:

"I often miss those evenings outside the conservatory."

I said I did too.

"You used to give me so much good advice. I often regret not having written it down."

To tell the truth I couldn't remember any advice, but let it pass. She seemed to realize this and added in explanation, "Perhaps it was more thinking aloud than actual advice, but I still regret not having written it down so I wouldn't forget. For instance, the story about the man who bathed in soda water because he thought it would increase his fertility. That's one story I won't forget, of course."

I said surely I'd told her something more useful than that.

"You also taught me how to tell a wild duck from a domestic one. The wild duck has red feet, you said, and they are smaller than the feet of a domestic duck."

I expressed surprise. She smiled.

"Actually, I've been looking for wild ducks with red feet for years but can never find any."

We both burst out laughing.

It was so nice to see her again and reminisce about the past that evening. She offered me port with my cheese but I found the Muscat so refreshing that we opened another bottle and sat up late, gazing at the stars and the moon and forgetting ourselves. Her husband had long since gone to bed and the girl who waited on us had said good night. A warm breeze blew off the lake, pattering the leaves of the vine and the sycamore beside the veranda. In the twilight I thought I could hear the merry tinkling of bells.

"Write to me, Disa," she said suddenly. "Anything that comes to mind. It doesn't matter what."

The following morning was warm, the air a hazy yellow, as we drove away from the house after breakfasting with Marilyn and her husband in the kitchen. I waved to them through the rear window and resolved to write to her on the way to Iceland.

I was awakened this morning by a crash as the chambermaid dropped a tray on the floor outside my door. It was nearly eight o'clock. Someone came to help her, a man from the sound of his voice, and they talked in low voices as they hurriedly cleared up pieces of glass, teaspoons and crockery. Something must have upset the girl, as I hadn't been aware of any motion. Perhaps this is her first voyage.

This incident reminded me of the old waiter at Boulestin's restaurant and I decided to put my memories down on paper and send them to little Marilyn, as my promise to write to her was still uppermost in my mind. I sat up in bed; I was feeling relaxed and when I saw the grayness outside and the lowering sky it didn't occur to me to get up. I felt contented, and even though the memories of the first months at Boulestin's all seemed to crowd in on me at once, this didn't disturb my peace of mind.

To the eyes of a girl from Kopasker, the voyage to Liverpool in 1936 was quite an adventure, and the train journey to London was no less strange and unfamiliar. This morning, as I recalled those days, what cheered me up most was the memory of the way Boulestin and Mrs. Brown welcomed me. I was astonished to see my employer at the station and had difficulty in finding the right words. He greeted me with a fatherly air, explaining that he had promised his friend Sivertsen to keep an eye on me. Just as I was about to stammer out some words of thanks in my broken English, Mrs. Brown beckoned to a porter and took my arm.

"You're staying with me," she said decisively.

"Watch out for the rent she charges!" whispered Boulestin teasingly, and they both burst out laughing.

No, those memories didn't disturb me, though it was strange that at the same time my thoughts should turn to my brother Kari, who now lives in Seattle in America and whom I haven't seen since he was a boy. Perhaps it was Father's letter that reminded me of him.

"Kari has been accepted by a respected university in the United States," he wrote to me after I had been at Boulestin's for about six months. "He's way ahead of his contemporaries and it looks as if he'll graduate top of his year from the Akureyri High School this spring."

There was no question that Father was proud of his son, though reading between the lines, I could sense the regret when he wrote that now they would be alone in the house, "the old couple," as he put it.

Kari sends me a Christmas card every year with photographs of the family, along with a duplicated report in English about what they have been up to during the past year. I find this American custom rather odd, but always keep his cards all the same. I'm glad he's doing well for himself.

My thoughts wandered to and fro in this way while I nestled under the covers and it was only when I reached for a pen and paper that I realized that I had forgotten a significant detail in my account of my evening with Marilyn. It had completely slipped my mind until now. I couldn't help smiling, the oversight was so extraordinary, but I was suddenly overcome with a sense of vulnerability. Was my memory no longer to be trusted? Was I going prematurely senile? I lay back and recalled the evening again.

As the meal went on, I couldn't help feeling that little Marilyn wanted to tell me something. Unable to sit still, she fidgeted in her chair and kept a close watch to see whether the girl who was waiting on us was within earshot. Finally, when the girl had gone to wash up and we could hear the constant sound of running water and the clattering of cutlery, she composed herself in her chair and said quietly:

"You'll probably have noticed that Bill and I don't have any children."

This question—or, rather, statement—took me by surprise. When I answered, prompted by my conscience, that I hadn't given it a thought, I could tell from her expression that she didn't believe me.

"I can't have children," she said. "We've been trying for years."

I have never been comfortable with this sort of conversation and avoid it if I possibly can, either by changing the subject or retreating if there are more than two people present. Yesterday evening, however, there was no escape, either through word or action. So I said something to the effect that they seemed to me to have a lot in common, which mattered more. Children were lovely, I said, but no guarantee of a happy marriage.

She listened to me in silence, but it didn't escape me that her revelation contained more than just a plea for sympathy. As soon as I had finished speaking she leaned over to me and whispered: "We've been thinking about adopting a child, but

I'm of two minds, Disa. I don't know whether it's right. Bill says it's up to me to decide, but I simply can't make up my mind. Oh, Disa, I don't think I've ever been so confused."

I felt uncomfortable, but asked her all the same what it was that worried her.

At first she said she had mainly been worried that the child would sense that they weren't its parents—"you know what I mean," she added, "biological parents or whatever it's called"—but lately she had been plagued by the suspicion that the children available for people in her position were mostly from problem families and could therefore themselves turn out to be difficult.

"Of course, I don't know anything about heredity," she said, "but I can't help having these worries."

She fell silent and we listened to the wind stirring the odd leaf in the trees, as if it were looking for something it couldn't find. Then I cleared my throat and admitted that it was difficult to give advice in these matters.

"But I suppose there are many different reasons why mothers have to give up their children," I said. "And I don't feel qualified to judge them."

At that moment her cat came out on to the veranda, jumped in her lap and mewed plaintively. Having spoken her piece, she changed the subject, but I had begun to think of tomorrow with trepidation. The trip to Scotland made me anxious, the thought of leaving behind the calm, rolling fields for the ice-scoured Border hills, the rocky streams in the gullies, the sight of sheep trying to cross them. It made me think of Iceland and again I questioned whether I was ready for this trip.

A white canvas had been hung over the street where it ended in a square, and tents in every color of the rainbow clustered near the park. When we left the train and headed for Earl's Court, I could see nothing but the tallest tents above the milling crowd of people, which was hardly surprising since this was the circus's last evening in London. It was past nine o'clock and I was taken aback at first by how many people had brought along their children, some of them very young, but told myself that the weather was lovely and unusually warm for the middle of September.

"An Indian summer," Boulestin had said that morning when he popped his head into the kitchen. "I even slept with the window open last night."

Mrs. Brown couldn't resist teasing him a little, as we both knew how easily he caught chills.

"You did sleep in a scarf and hat, though, didn't you?" she asked, shaking with suppressed mirth.

He took the joke well, then said to me: "Well, Miss Jonsdottir from Iceland, aren't you going to allow yourself any fun before autumn comes? I'm beginning to feel like a slave driver."

It was quite right that I hadn't gone out much during the three months since my arrival in England, but then I didn't have much free time at the restaurant on Leicester Square. Sometimes the pressure was almost too much for me but I never saw any reason to complain. The Restaurant Boulestin was unsurpassed by any other restaurant in London in those days. Among the people who flocked there were actors, politicians, aristocracy and prominent businessmen, mingling with guests from the finest hotels in the city, particularly the Ritz and Savoy. It wasn't unusual for the staff of one of these hotels to have to beg for a table at the last minute, so busy was the restaurant almost every day, and we generally tried to squeeze them in, though sometimes we couldn't do anything to help.

"But it's for Sir James Hetherington," they would cry. "He'll be accompanied by . . . You must be able to fit them in."

"Sorry."

But I had that evening off and had decided to go to the circus with Julie Smith, one of the girls I worked with. We told Boulestin and Mrs. Brown of our plan.

"Good," he said.

"Yes, but do be careful of the monkeys," she added.

They roared with laughter, but I was a bit slow on the uptake and didn't immediately realize that she must have been referring to men.

In one tent clowns stood on their heads, while next door a man swallowed fire, tossed a dagger up into the air and caught it again, sticking out his tongue to embellish his act. We lingered in front of the clowns' tent, then watched the strongest man in the world offer to arm-wrestle members of the audience. When we had taken a look at what was happening in every tent, we bought ice creams and sat on a bench in the park. Julie was easygoing and we didn't talk much as we ate the ices, though of course we laughed at the clowns and the lion tamer, who pretended to have lost his lion, and wondered aloud whether it was going to rain. No doubt we could have hit upon a more worthy topic of conversation but the absurdity of the circus charmed us with its farcical illusions and shameless behavior, with all its public grotesquerie, which doesn't really take anyone in but nevertheless manages to win most people over.

When we finally stood up, Julie looked at her watch and saw that it was time for her to head off home as she had farther to go than I did. Before we said good-bye, she asked if I was absolutely sure about going home alone by underground. I told her not to worry about me. She hurried across the park and out of the northern gate, but I decided to walk back past the circus tents on my way to the station.

No sooner had I entered the sea of humanity again than I sensed that something had changed from earlier in the evening. People seemed jittery as they thronged down the alley toward the white canvas over the square or hurried away to take refuge amid the clowns and other freaks. I was curious and let myself be carried along with the flow, all the way to the benches which had been lined up before a low stage under the canvas. People fought for the seats closest to the stage, some elbowing their way through as if they had forgotten all their manners. I took a seat on the second row from the back, near the middle.

"Bring on the freak!" I heard people calling as I sat down and at that moment I caught sight of a sign to the right of the stage. "A fabulous creature from the African jungle," said the sign. "Man or beast? Dr. Kivan will reveal the truth to you."

Draped in front of the stage was a purple curtain which might once have graced a cinema but was now a mere rag, ripped right through in one place. A little boy crept up to the stage to peep through the tear but his father caught him at the last minute and jerked him back to his seat. There was a distant thunder and everyone looked at the sky; somewhere there must be a downpour, but not a drop fell where we sat.

I looked at my watch. The show was supposed to have started ten minutes ago but there was no sign of either Dr. Kivan or the so-called fabulous creature from Africa. A muttering rose from the crowd, children were getting restless and whimpering with tiredness. I couldn't understand why their parents hadn't taken them home to bed hours ago. I'd only become aware of my own weariness when I sat down, and so decided to leave and make my way home. But at that moment the curtain was raised and Dr. Kivan appeared before us in all his glory. He stood, legs apart, at the front of the stage in white breeches, high black leather boots, and a shiny serge jacket with a belt around his waist, a whip hanging from one side and a copper-green key from the other. In spite of the costume, the doctor looked flabby, with rounded shoulders and greasy skin, his eyes small and weak beneath his white cap, like the eyes of a pig. They peered searchingly around the tent, and some people found his gaze so uncomfortable that they dropped their own eyes. A few stared stubbornly back. Then Dr. Kivan smirked and slowly twisted up the ends of his waxed mustache.

"Dangers lurk everywhere," he began at last in a harsh, artificially deepened voice. "In the most unlikely places. When least expected. Without the slightest warning, they will dig their claws into us like savage beasts, mercilessly— even on a warm, pleasant evening like tonight . . ."

A buzz of anticipation went through the tent, as intended.

"I am not talking about lions or tigers, or poisonous snakes or crocodiles, not even the black savages who chased me for days through the Gobi desert. All these dangers were foresee-able."

He had begun to pace up and down on the stage as he spoke, and I noticed that he had a limp. The crowd's eyes followed him like a slow-swinging pendulum, their attention glued to him in silent unison. Finally he stopped again, hooked his thumbs in his belt and said with false nonchalance, as if he were commenting on a minor change in the weather:

"Nothing took me by surprise but the monsters, deformed creatures which I hadn't known existed. Beasts which are not beasts, men which are not human." He had gradually lowered his voice, but now he almost shouted: "Monstrosities, I tell you, monstrosities!"

Naturally the audience was startled by his yell. Some gripped their neighbors, then began to laugh and whisper together to ease the tension.

"You laugh. You think it's amusing. Let's see whether you are still as carefree when you yourselves have looked into the eyes of deformity."

He walked with slow, deliberate steps toward the back of the stage where a cage could be dimly discerned in the dark shadows. At first I wasn't aware of any movement inside, but when Dr. Kivan raised his whip and cracked the lash, a little creature barely three feet high sprang up and gave a hair-raising shriek. The doctor stumbled back, as if he hadn't expected this reception; the audience gasped.

"You threaten me!" he cried. "Will you restrain yourself if I let you out?"

The only answer he received was a pitiful wail like a dog that has been kicked.

"Very well, since you promise to be good. But don't think I'm going to undo the chain."

He strutted over to the cage, brandishing the key which

had been hanging from his belt, leaned forward and half-opened the door. Then he walked cautiously to the front of the stage.

"Come here!" he ordered.

Dead silence.

"Come here!"

There was a rattle of chains and a dwarfish creature staggered out of the cage and came to a halt in the middle of the stage, a couple of yards from the showman.

Dwarfish *creature,* I say, but should of course have said straightaway that it was just an ordinary dwarf. Admittedly, he was dressed in an outlandish costume, a skirt made from bones—thigh bones, I guessed—and a green cloak, which hung down from his shoulders. On his head perched a colorful crown of feathers. His face was also painted, red, yellow and black; it was large with an oddly high forehead, round bulging eyes and ears so tiny they could hardly be seen, like shriveled prunes.

The doctor looked out solemnly over the audience and made a long speech about how he had captured "the monster" in the African jungle and brought it back to England. Then he told of his attempts to train the creature (I remember quite clearly that he used the word "train" and not "teach") and finally offered to show the audience what progress he had made. The whip whined and the dwarf was made to stand on one foot, jump up in the air, poke out his tongue, grimace and stick his backside out at the audience. They laughed, their children wide awake now, kept going by the excitement. The whiplash sang ever higher and Dr. Kivan's orders grew louder and louder until without warning he folded his arms and said contemptuously:

"Well, it's clear that the beast has at least the intelligence of a dog."

Most people roared with laughter at his scorn but I noticed

that some were uneasy, as if they felt the fun was turning sour.

"You've behaved well enough this evening," said the showman. "I think you deserve to be let loose."

The audience gasped, stuck their heads together and giggled—behaving, in short, just as they were supposed to. The dwarf shook himself, but didn't move from his place.

"Do you suppose it can speak?" asked Dr. Kivan. "Would you believe I have managed to teach it to speak? Wouldn't that be a miracle?"

He glared at the dwarf.

"Thirteen!"

No doubt he chose this number deliberately.

"Repeat after me," he ordered: "Thirteen!"

The dwarf screeched.

Dr. Kivan stepped menacingly toward him, raised his whip in the air and repeated: "Thirteen!"

It was then that the little creature suddenly began to screech in Icelandic.

"Argara thargara!" he wailed. "Kettir, kettir . . ."

The audience gasped, but I was stunned. I suddenly felt as if I were part of someone else's nightmare.

"You can hear it's a wild beast," said Dr. Kivan. "Thirteen! I said, thirteen!"

"Fir . . . Fir . . ."

"Good, good. Thirteen!"

"Firt . . ."

"Thirteen!"

The whip cracked over the dwarf's head, touching the feathers, which fluttered in the draft.

"Thirteen! I said, thirteen!"

"Firteen . . ."

"Firteen," he imitated the wretched creature mockingly. "Firteen . . ."

Then he bellowed as if his life depended on it: "I said thirteen! Thirteen, I said!"

At the same moment he hurled the lash at the dwarf, who wailed with pain and with a great bound ran at the doctor, who fell flat on his face. The dwarf rushed to the front of the stage, scowling and hissing and finally spitting out a streak of flame at the audience.

When he braced himself to leap down among them with the fire streaming from his mouth, many people were terrified, jumping out of their seats and stampeding in panic, frantic parents grabbing their children, everyone barging past one another with no thought of consideration. I allowed myself to be borne out into the street with the throng, as otherwise I would have been trampled. Some people did lose their footing in the pandemonium and when I tried to help a middle-aged woman to her feet I was knocked down too. I landed heavily as I had barely room to put out a protective hand, and couldn't immediately get up. It was then that he reached out his hand to me. He had been pushed over as well. I looked up into his face. It was calm amidst all the madness and there was a smile in his eyes. I had seen him somewhere before but couldn't place him.

"Jakob Himmelfarb," he introduced himself when we had regained our feet. His accent was German.

I was slow to reply.

"I sometimes eat at the Restaurant Boulestin," he said with a humorous glint in his eye. "Could it be that I've seen you there?"

I don't remember how I answered, but suspected he might have noticed me when Boulestin had asked me to help out with the waitressing. Though I didn't mention that I regarded this job as beneath me.

He had taken my arm and I made no objection, even though I was perfectly capable of walking without help.

"Would some refreshment help?"

"He was Icelandic," I stammered.

"I'm sorry?"

"The dwarf. He spoke Icelandic. Cats, he wailed. Cats in Icelandic."

He laughed.

"So that was what it was. Icelandic."

There was a clap of thunder above our heads.

Then it began to rain.

"Would you like to come to a concert with me on Saturday?" he had asked just before we parted.

I was over eager to answer.

"Yes," I blurted out, without asking any questions. Neither of us could help smiling. I blushed.

He said he thought the concert began at one o'clock.

"I don't have to work until the evening," I added awkwardly.

"I'll ring you tomorrow to confirm."

I didn't walk home from the station, I floated. Mrs. Brown was still awake. She couldn't help noticing the metamorphosis.

"What on earth has happened? Is there something you want to tell me?"

The following day was wet and dreary but I didn't notice. Not until Mrs. Brown announced that she had decided to sell her old Vactrix vacuum cleaner and had paid for an advertisement in the Saturday paper.

"I'd completely forgotten that I've got to go to a funeral on

Saturday. Would you be a dear and answer the phone for me while I'm out? I'll be back by three."

I was overcome and all at once the weather seemed even drearier. Who would give that piece of old junk a second glance, even if it was useful once, before the Great War? But I didn't like to say this to her after all she had done for me.

When I told Jakob I wouldn't be able to come, he could hear my disappointment at once. So it shouldn't have been necessary for me to repeat myself so often.

"We'll just have to go another time," he said. "Good luck with the sale."

I thanked him.

"By the way, what did you say she was trying to sell?"

"An ancient Vactrix vacuum cleaner."

"A Vactrix? I say!"

We both laughed.

Mrs. Brown went out at midday on Saturday. She had hardly moved from the phone all morning but of course it had remained silent.

"Perhaps there's something wrong with it," she kept saying, picking up the receiver to make sure she could hear the tone.

"I don't understand this at all."

She had just left when the phone rang. I nearly jumped out of my skin, as I had been preoccupied with thoughts of the concert I was missing, but had recovered my composure by the time I answered.

"Good afternoon," said a squeaky male voice. "Am I right in thinking that you are advertising an electric Vactrix vacuum cleaner?"

I said he was.

"What luck. I've been looking out for a Vactrix in a good condition for months. It's as good as new, is it?"

"Yes," I replied. "There's hardly a scratch on it."

"What luck," he repeated. "And what do you want for it?"

I mentioned the price that Mrs. Brown had said, but was quick to add that I was prepared to be accommodating if necessary.

"Only four pounds and three shillings!" he exclaimed. "I hardly like to pay so little. Wouldn't five pounds be more like it?"

"That would be even better," I said. "If you would prefer . . ."

"We're agreed, then. Five pounds. I much prefer that. Five pounds. When can I fetch it?"

"Whenever you like."

"Now?"

"That would be fine."

"Good. I'll be along shortly. I don't live far away."

Shortly afterward there was a knock at the door.

"He didn't take long to arrive," I thought to myself. "Mrs. Brown will be pleased when she comes home." I had formed a mental picture of the buyer, a small man in his sixties, bald apart from a few straggling white hairs at the sides perhaps, with kind eyes. And this was what I was expecting when I opened the front door.

"Jakob!"

"I was just passing."

I didn't want to show how pleased I was to see him but knew he couldn't help noticing.

"Aren't you supposed to be at the concert now?"

"I would rather see you. I bought us lunch on the way. I hope you haven't eaten already ?"

He was carrying a paper bag and I automatically leaned over the threshold to peep inside. Fruit, cheese, bread, paté and red wine.

"Have you eaten?"

"No," I answered, finally coming to my senses sufficiently to invite him in.

Sitting at the little round table in the room which overlooked the square, we cut slices of pear and cheese to put on the bread and poured ourselves glasses of wine. Naturally, I forgot all about the vacuum cleaner and the little old man I had been waiting for, forgot him completely until Jakob said, "How are you getting on with selling the Vactrix vacuum cleaner?"

I was startled.

"He should have been here by now," I said, as if to myself.

"Who?"

I told him about the funny old man and the five pounds he had insisted on paying for the thing.

"Really? What was his name?"

I realized I had never asked his name.

"Young?"

"No, getting on. At least, from what I could hear."

"Rather a squeaky voice?"

I nodded.

"Like this?"

He altered his voice, sounding just like the old man on the phone. "In good condition? What luck. But four pounds and three shillings is nothing. Five, at least five pounds. I couldn't pay any less . . . ' "

"Jakob!" I cried, leaping up. "Shame on you!"

He dodged, shaking with laughter, and I chased him: "You tricked me . . . shame on you!" I shook him in high spirits and he put his arms round me playfully to restrain me. I struggled in his embrace and he crushed me against him until our lips met.

I couldn't tear myself away from him, unwilling to let this indescribable sense of well-being slip from my grasp.

I should have sensed that I was being warned. It should have been obvious to me, as I don't believe in coincidences and Dr. Kivan's farce must have been a bad omen. It would have been enough to have thanked him for his help, said good-bye and hurried home instead of sitting down with him in a café and losing myself in a treacherous happiness.

Perhaps it would have been better for me if I had listened when Mrs. Brown said: "I know it's none of my business but he's Jewish, isn't he?"

The end seemed inevitable, obvious even on the evening he proposed to me. If only I had remembered Dr. Kivan at that moment and the Icelandic dwarf which he persuaded people to believe was a monster, I would have understood that this was what the world had come to and everything would have been different. Everything.

Boulestin said little at first when I plucked up the courage to tell him that I was going to move to the country and stay there for the next few months.

"Where?" he asked.

"A summer cottage not far from Bath," I answered, without mentioning the fact that I intended to live there with Jakob.

He looked at me in silence for a while; I could see he was putting two and two together. However, he was too discreet to mention Jakob. Instead he said: "Maybe the work is too difficult for you."

I was so hurt and angry that I couldn't utter a word.

"If it is," he continued, "there's no hope of your ever being able to run a restaurant. It's not enough to show promise."

I was on the verge of answering him back but fortunately had the sense to bite back the words.

"When are you going?"

"In three weeks."

"Try to use them well," he said. "You won't learn anything about cooking once you've left town."

That he should dare to insinuate that I couldn't handle the work! I decided to show him what I was made of and refused to take a single day off during my last few weeks.

"Isn't this going a bit far?" asked Mrs. Brown, who knew what was going on.

"No one tells me that I can't cope with hard work," I answered.

Boulestin pretended hardly to notice me during those last days but now I suspect he was amused by my obstinacy. In fact, I'm sure he was.

Jakob tried to make me change my mind but I lost my temper with him. He was light-hearted in those days as he had just finished his doctoral thesis and was at last free to enjoy himself. He had taken on some proofreading for the University Press and was looking forward to getting out into the country. At first his happiness made me even grumpier but before I knew it I had started to laugh at his teasing.

I am ashamed to recall what a simpleton I was in those days, how blind I was. Of course, I loved Jakob more than words can tell, but what is love but a quest for disappointment? I was blind when I took leave of Mrs. Brown with a long embrace. Blind when I lied to my mother that I was going to Somerset for Boulestin.

Blind.

When we got talking after dinner, the first engineer began to enthuse about the car I had arrived in. He was clearly surprised that I should know anything about it, though I explained to him that this was quite by chance. It was obvious that he was very keen on machines and cars and he embarked on a rather lengthy description of the spare parts and carburetors he had bought while in port. I nodded out of politeness as he was a nice chap. When he turned the conversation to the *Gullfoss*'s engines and invited me down to the engine room, I didn't know what else to do but go with him.

We were down there for some time and I can honestly say that I enjoyed myself. The engines roared with a confidence-inspiring steadiness, unaffected by the whims of the world, by disasters or changes of mood. The smell of oil mingled with sea salt, filling me with courage.

As we emerged from the engine room, we were greeted by the clinking of glasses and crockery, and an unpleasant reek of smoke. The engineer invited me to sit with him in the smoking saloon and I couldn't really do anything but accompany him, even though I had no interest in consorting with the people sitting in there. Supper had passed without strain as I had the good luck to end up between two Danes who spoke neither Icelandic nor English. To make things easier for myself I lied to them at the beginning of the meal that I didn't speak Danish. They were therefore perfectly agreeable dinner companions.

Now, however, I was defenseless. We had no sooner entered the saloon than the engineer began to introduce me to one passenger after another. Till now I had managed to keep myself to myself, avoiding having anything to do with any of them, but now there was no escape. No doubt he thought he was doing me a favor, assuming that my lack of sociability stemmed from shyness.

"She knows about cars," he said more often than once to break the ice. Unfortunately, he was successful.

"Cars, hee hee," tittered a young woman with a pale complexion and a white hat, her long fingers toting a cigarette-holder, which made them seem even thinner and whiter. The man with her began a long monologue about a Studebaker he apparently meant to buy shortly. I bore with the conversation which followed his declaration, trying to show the proper politeness so that the engineer wouldn't think I was arrogant. All the same, I guessed from his expression that he read my mind and sympathized. But perhaps it was only my imagination. He took me to a table in the corner and asked whether I wasn't in need of refreshment after all this car talk. Then he turned to wave to a waiter.

I had no sooner sat down than the doctor of medieval literature slumped down in the chair opposite me. There was something about his manner which I didn't like, a pathetic look that I hadn't noticed before and couldn't put my finger on but which immediately put my back up.

"I'm finished," he announced to me, continuing to drain his glass. "Finished," he repeated. "Fini."

"That's a shame," I answered, instead of keeping my mouth shut.

"Three years in Copenhagen and two in Edinburgh. And my father and mother think I've taken my exams. They think I'm the best-educated man in Iceland."

"And that you've discovered the author of *Egil's Saga,* isn't that so?"

I looked around. The engineer had disappeared. I would have to wait.

"My father's a fisherman. He's a fisherman," he repeated, mumbling into his glass. "A fisherman," as if he had only just realized the fact.

The waiter brought me a glass of sherry.

"Ingolfur will be back in a moment. He just had to step up to the bridge."

"My mother works in a bakery. I'm the eldest. Siggi is twenty and my sister Edda was confirmed this spring. They're all going to meet me on the docks. All of them. And my father will put his fist on my shoulder and say: 'we're proud of you, my boy.' 'Dr. Hallgrimur Palsson,' my mother will say solemnly. 'Soon to be professor.' "

He laughed, then his face crumpled and he began to sob.

"I haven't completed a single exam in the last three years."

He was sorry for himself. My goodness, was he sorry for himself.

"And they've scrimped and saved. All these years they've been saving up."

There were two couples sitting at the next table. I noticed that the women were eavesdropping.

"I'm going to drown myself tonight. I'm going to throw myself overboard before we get home."

His declaration clearly worried the women at the next table. They nudged their husbands. But I had had enough.

"That's a good idea," I said. "What are you waiting for?"

He looked stunned.

"I'm going to *drown* myself," he repeated. "Put an end to my life."

His voice was slurred but he managed nevertheless to pronounce "put an end to my life" with something approaching solemnity.

"Yes, well, shouldn't you be getting a move on? The weather's fine and the sea's calm. Not bad weather for killing yourself."

I stood up. He looked like a dog which had just been kicked.

"How could you say that? How could you say that to me?"

The couples at the next table put their heads together. I guessed what they were whispering when I saw their expressions. But what did they know? What experience did they have of boys like this?

I knew what sort of person I had been sitting with. I knew the type.

Franz Himmelfarb owned two factories, one in Berlin, the other in Dusseldorf. He also owned a book shop which stocked antiquarian and rare books, an abattoir, a partnership in a newspaper, and a firm selling umbrellas and sunshades.

"Of course they're rich," said Mrs. Brown. "They're Jewish."

Jakob had little interest in his father's business and seldom mentioned it.

"The only difference between an umbrella and a sunshade is the color," he once said. "No doubt Father would be delighted if the Lord were to invent something new for people to shelter from."

I never met his parents but judging from photographs Jakob was the image of his father. Yet he had his mother's mouth—a beautiful woman with large eyes and wavy hair. I once asked him about their religion.

"They have assimilated," he answered, smiling. "They have the same representative to the Almighty as you—old Luther."

As for himself, he said he believed in the sun, moon and stars.

His doctoral thesis was on Blake's poetry.

I care not whether a man is Good or Evil; all that I care
Is whether he is a Wise Man or a Fool.
Go! put off Holiness,
And put on Intellect.

How impressive it sounded when he quoted it. The Great War was the result of stupidity and misunderstanding, he explained, not wickedness, treachery or cunning. "Wretched fools," he said of the Continental heads of state, "cockerels who competed to see who could crow loudest on their dunghills until they could no longer avoid clashing." And that's how it had always been—since history began—though ignorant historians did their utmost to define the lunacy in terms of good and evil.

We were sitting out on the veranda under a blue tarpaulin which we had hung over it shortly after our arrival. It began to rain but we remained dry and unconcerned under the canvas, watching the drops forming rivulets along the gutters in the road, and the dusk falling silently over the valley. Jakob leaned back in his chair, the song of his typewriter silenced, the hare which I had bought that morning cooking in a pot on the primitive stove. We feared nothing under that blue canopy, nothing whatsoever. Wars and battles belonged to history and there was little danger of them being repeated here.

Steam rose from the earth after the rain. He put his arms around me, his eyes large and brown, his fingers long and tender on my breasts.

"Out here?" I asked.

"Show him the way," he whispered.

"Here?"

"Stroke him . . . Show him the way . . ."

Brown eyes, I think, though sometimes I seem to see other eyes staring at me when I try to remember him. Sometimes all I can see is his silhouette in my mind. Sometimes just his beret with no face under it. Then I become afraid and sit up in bed with a jerk. "Anthony," I call, but have forgotten what I meant to say to him by the time he comes to me with the sleep still in his eyes.

It was a warm spring. We generally sat outside on the veranda in the late afternoon, waiting for dusk to fall on the day's efforts. I remember once hearing laughter carried to us from somewhere in the valley. This was at the end of May. We both listened as the wind wafted it over to us in intermittent waves which were sometimes difficult to pick up. It was like listening to a tune from a hurdy-gurdy man carried a long distance on the breeze. The wind would drop for a moment and nothing could be heard, so I thought the girl had stopped (we were both convinced it was a girl laughing), then at that moment the wind would change direction and without warning the laughter would sound again.

"She laughs like you, Disa."

"I don't laugh like that."

"Exactly the same."

"Me?"

"Just that sort of rippling laughter."

"Not like that."

Jakob imitated the laugh: "Tee, hee, heeheehee . . ."

"I don't laugh like that."

"Will you marry me?"

The breeze caressed our cheeks and the night drew its
blanket over us. We embraced again and again, unable to be
apart, his breath was my breath, his heart beat in my breast.

The following morning I went to the telephone exchange
in Paulton to ring my mother. It was sunny when I set off but
by the time I reached the outskirts of the village it had begun
to rain. I was cycling and hadn't brought a coat, so I was
soaked to the skin in a matter of seconds. There was no wind
but the raindrops were big and heavy and my dress soon
clung to my body. By the road into the village there was a
small church and I remember the vicar standing in the doorway as I cycled past. I think he waved to me with a smile. I also
remember the butcher, a friend of mine, standing cheerfully
at the window of his shop as I coasted past, but perhaps that is
just my imagination. I enjoyed the feel of the rain on my face,
which was red and hot after the sunshine of the last few days.

It took more than two hours to get a connection to
Kopasker.

"Disa, is that you? Is something wrong?"

"There's nothing wrong, Mother. I've got engaged."

Silence. Crackling on the line.

"I said I've got engaged."

"What did you say, child?"

I gabbled on nineteen to the dozen despite the poor connection. "We're getting married this autumn," I told her,
"when we get back to London. Jakob, he's called, Jakob Himmelfarb, a German. I love him, I tell you, love him so much
you wouldn't believe it, Mother. And it's so beautiful here in
the countryside, there's a little stream by the garden (which
isn't so much a garden as a meadow) and the grass has started
to turn green and the birds have begun to sing all day long
for our amusement. I get butter, cheese, eggs, chickens and
ducks from the farm farther up the valley, the people there

are so dependable and easy to get along with." I also told her about the butcher and the little restaurant beside the library where I cooked three evenings a week. "Butler's Tavern, it's called," but I didn't mention that I was forbidden to cook anything except traditional English food since the owner received complaints. I told her that Jakob and I had been to London twice that year—"God, how expensive everything is there compared to here, Mother. A pound of butter costs . . . and the cheese isn't nearly as good. But it was fun to see Julie and some of the other staff." However, I didn't mention the falling out between Boulestin and myself, though Mrs. Brown had told me that he was ready to take me back in the autumn. "But perhaps we'll come to Iceland first. Yes, Jakob has suggested that it might not be a bad idea as things stand. Oh, Mother, I'm so happy."

Silence.

"Mother?"

I thought the connection had been lost.

"Mother, are you there?"

"I was under the impression you were in the country-side under Boulestin's protection," I heard her say. "How come you've never told us before about this—what's he called again?—this Jakob? You said you were there for Boulestin . . ."

"Oh, Mother . . ."

"You deceived us. Your parents. And now you claim you're engaged. Are you out of your mind, child? Is there something wrong with you? Deceived us, your parents. And now you say you're getting married this autumn. You're out of your mind . . ."

I had begun to cry.

"Mother, you don't understand . . ."

"No, I don't understand you. I don't understand how you could treat us like that. After everything we've done for you.

Your father . . . And then you go behind our backs. This sort of behavior leads to nothing but unhappiness. Nothing but unhappiness, Asdis."

The tune from the traveling hurdy-gurdy man, apparently seamless at first, then falling apart. The notes are lost when the wind drops, becoming scattered and in the end forgetting one another, lost in the void. Lonely notes drifting through the emptiness, futile—completely futile.

In July David, Jakob's younger brother, announced his imminent arrival. His letter was waiting for us when we came home after a day's walk in the woods; I remember being surprised that the letter should be from him as the handwriting on the envelope was so elegant that I had assumed the sender was a woman. The envelope was blue and so was the paper. Light blue.

We were tired and happy that day after a long walk and a dip in a little lake we had come across and had completely to ourselves. The lake—or rather pond—was hidden in a leafy clearing and Jakob amused himself by diving below the surface, swimming up to me underwater and seizing my toes. At first I was anxious, thinking he had been under for too long and imagining that he had got caught in the weeds at the bottom and couldn't get free. Then my toes were pinched and I burst out laughing with relief when he surfaced and took me in his arms. We ate a late lunch on the bank of the pond, cold omelette, smoked salmon and cheese, and drank a translucent red wine which slipped down the throat without troubling the brain cells. After the meal we dozed and when we awoke the shadows were lengthening and the flat rocks of the bank had grown cool to the touch. We strolled home accompanied by the diffident rays of the evening sun.

"He intends to stay for one night," said Jakob after reading the letter. "And he will not be alone."

He was fond of his brother and looked forward to seeing him, as well as being curious to meet his girlfriend. David seemed to be madly in love with her and Jakob's smile became almost paternal as he read his brother's description of the girl, so sincere and ingenuous were his comments.

They arrived on Saturday, shortly after midday. We watched them walk up the drive to the house, David carrying a small suitcase in one hand and holding the girl's hand in the other. She wore a long white skirt, white blouse and a white hat on her head, a tall, slim figure, gliding along like a moonbeam. Jakob kissed his brother on both cheeks and I did the same even though I didn't know him; he was a good-looking young man, more delicately built than his brother and not as tall. The girl, whose name was Anna, greeted me with a weak handshake but Jakob was quick to give her a welcome kiss. David fussed around her like a humble servant and Jakob and I gave each other sideways glances and smiled, as it was almost funny to watch the boy's behavior.

"Would you like to sit here in the shade? I'll fetch a chair for you. Is the seat comfortable enough? Would you like me to fetch a cushion? Are you comfortable now?"

She offered to help me in the kitchen, and when I declined sat in the shade on the veranda and asked David to light her a cigarette. She smoked one after another and David leaped up at regular intervals to relieve her of the stub and empty the ashtray. She caressed his neck whenever he bent down to her and nibbled his earlobe teasingly after whispering something to him which doubtless wasn't meant for our ears. Perhaps she thought we wouldn't notice but somehow I'm not convinced. I thought he blushed.

When Jakob suggested we take a stroll down to the river and over to the next valley, she said she'd prefer to stay behind and rest. David was quick to decide to stay behind with her. I looked over my shoulder when we reached the river. She was still sitting in the shade on the veranda, David at her side watching us. For some reason I felt sure they would go inside the moment we were out of sight.

Though I say so myself, supper was delicious. I had pulled out all the stops for David's sake. First we ate vegetable soup, then blue cheese and ham which I had baked in a pastry crust, then finally pigeons served with prunes. We drank a young red wine which Jakob had picked up on our last visit to London; it had a pleasant flavor. We tried to talk as little as possible about the situation in Germany, but naturally couldn't avoid it altogether. The girl took no part in the conversation, keeping silent. I don't remember how the talk turned to Catholics, but Jakob said he had heard that the German government was continuing to charge monks with sexual deviancy. He didn't hide his opinion but when his brother David opened his mouth to agree with him, his girlfriend said in a teasing voice:

"Since when have you been so interested in monks?"

She sat between Jakob and me at the round table in the sitting room, flirting a little with Jakob, getting in her laugh before David or me whenever he made an amusing comment, and flattering him at every opportunity. Her parents had moved to Namibia before the Nazis came to power but she didn't mention them to Jakob or me. I had gathered from David's letters that she herself was a student, though it was a bit unclear.

She smoked the odd cigarette during the meal, blowing the smoke to one side. At first David made sure that she wasn't put to the trouble of reaching for a cigarette and lighting it herself but as the meal went on he stopped noticing when she extended her fingers toward the packet. The food and wine had filled him with unexpected vigor and he prattled on, grilling me about Icelandic horses, as he was apparently a keen rider. He was cheerful and unsuspecting when Jakob began to ask him how everybody was at home in Munich.

"And how is your friend Lore?"

David took his brother's question literally, answering that he had met his childhood friend and her sister two weeks before when they were in London and had lunch with them.

"It began to rain while we were eating," he said, "and her sister was worried that she would get wet on the way home and Lore started to tease her and we laughed and laughed for no particular reason, just like old times."

Anna knew Jakob was enjoying himself at her expense. Her expression changed swiftly.

"Lore has always been so warm and fun," said Jakob. "And there's nothing wrong with her looks either."

I nudged him. He realized he had gone too far and tried to make amends but failed miserably: "I don't know how you always get these beautiful girls . . ."

The three of us ate every last mouthful of the pigeon but Anna appeared to have lost her appetite, merely prodding at each breast a couple of times before putting down her knife and fork. I could see that she was in the mood for revenge.

We drank coffee at the table since we didn't feel like moving. Darkness had fallen outside but inside it was warm and cozy in the light of the candles and the flickering glow from the hearth. How the conversation turned to swimming, I don't remember; I may have mentioned the pond where we had been taking dips for the last few days and the rocks on the bank which were hot by day but swiftly cooled as the sun got lower in the sky. I may have begun talking about the pond but it was Anna who suddenly cleared her throat and leaned forward in her seat.

"I adore swimming," she declared. "Simply adore it. Even during a civil war."

She looked at David.

"You remember what I wrote to you from San Sebastián, darling, don't you?"

David hung his head.

"It was so gorgeous by the beach," she continued. "After lunch everyone hurried down there because the more people went swimming, the more likely it was that someone would have a chance to escape. You known—refugees trying to swim over the border to France. Pretending to be on their summer holiday like us. It's perhaps shameful to admit it but we all found it exciting too. The Spanish guards always noticed them because they swam too quickly. Couldn't hold themselves back."

"What happened then?" asked Jakob in an expressionless voice.

"Well, the guards began to shoot. And we raced for the beach, swimming as fast as we could, and ran up on to the hot sand until there was no one left in the water except the fugitives. The end of the game was simple. It was sad. They never missed."

We sat in silence for a while. The fire crackled. But she hadn't finished.

"I know David doesn't want me to talk about it but we never saw the bodies, fortunately. The current carried them away toward Bordeaux, the very place they had been trying to get to in the first place."

She slept late the following morning. When she awoke, they came to say good-bye. David was subdued. Jakob kissed him on both cheeks and patted him on the back.

We breathed more easily once they had left the house.

I have often wondered whether I was genuinely pleased for my sister Jorunn when she wrote to me about her forthcoming marriage to Gunnar Olafsson, a chemist. I didn't know the man but judging by her description you would have thought he could walk on water. It didn't bother me but I found it strange that she didn't ask my opinion at all about the marriage. Admittedly, she had mentioned Gunnar two or three times in her letters, but not in a way that prepared me for a wedding in just a few months' time. I'd like to emphasize that it never occurred to me that she should need my consent—quite the contrary—but all the same it took me by surprise that she didn't even ask my opinion. I would have thought we were close enough that she wouldn't have chosen to tell me the news in a way which amounted to a public announcement. I have to admit I was quite upset.

At the same time I had given her clear hints about my feelings for Jakob. Naturally, I didn't go so far as to tell her in so many words that we were "living in sin," as they called it then, and I convinced myself that my caution was because I didn't want to get her into trouble. However, I realized later that underneath I had not entirely trusted her. And when I read her letter I was convinced that I had been right.

I was particularly annoyed by the postscript. She had obviously written the letter before I rang Mother and told her that I was engaged to Jakob but had not yet posted it.

P.S. Mother told me about your conversation yesterday. As you know, she is at her wits' end. I tried to calm her down but it wasn't any good. Father didn't say much. Let me know if there is anything I can do to help . . .

At least she had had the sense to rewrite the letter, crossing out the description of her trip with Gunnar up north to Kopasker—"I'm so glad Mother took to him so readily, they were the best of friends right away"—and cut down the tedious account of what a good family he came from. "Olafur, my prospective father-in-law, studied medicine with Father but I didn't find out until recently . . ."

She, the angel. I, the black sheep.

"You must give the impression that you're married," Mrs. Brown had advised me before we went to Somerset. "People in the provinces don't approve of unmarried couples living together. Any more than anywhere else . . ."

"You haven't been living together this winter, have you?" wrote Jorunn. "Mother thinks you have but I told her it couldn't possibly be true."

Pretending that she was trying to help me!

No, I didn't find it easy to be pleased for her when she wrote about her forthcoming marriage to Gunnar Olafsson, chemist.

Who can blame me?

I got to know Anthony early in '38, when Jakob and I had been in Somerset only a few months. He lived a short distance away from us at a small country lodge owned by his family, called, if I remember right, Whitewood Hall. Now the lodge and its flourishing, fertile estate have been forfeited, run through their hands like so much else. When passing Whitewood Hall I would frequently stop and admire the house. I'd get off my bicycle, lay it on the grass or lean it up against the solid stone wall and walk up to the gate or sit down on a tree stump outside it. The building itself was a delight to the eyes and so were the lawns around it, mown as closely as a Persian rug. Near at hand they were a brilliant green but over by the house they took on a bluish hue and sometimes the house looked like an island in a lake. I used to chew a stalk of grass or do nothing but gaze and imagine what it would be like to live in a house like that, seeing myself descending the broad sweep of the staircase in the morning, stretching toward the growing light, opening the window and inhaling the scent of newly mown grass, listening to the birdsong.

Later, when Anthony rescued me from Iceland, he told me

for the first time that he had noticed me outside the gate more than once. He also mumbled, half-embarrassed, that he had often fetched a telescope to watch me.

Anthony lived with his two aunts in the house. Neither of them had the slightest sense of humor, which might explain why he was such a frequent visitor to Jakob and me. He would invariably appear shortly before supper, bearing a bottle of wine or a little something for me, cheese or eggs from the old tenant farm or a volume from his library, usually poetry. He and Jakob had known each other since Jakob's first term at Oxford but my acquaintance with Anthony went deeper from the very beginning.

Once I said to Jakob.

"You know Shirley Jones?" Shirley Jones was the daughter of our neighbor, a pretty, amusing girl. "I think Shirley Jones has a bit of a crush on our friend Anthony. Perhaps we should invite them to a meal together?"

I was surprised by how unenthusiastic Jakob was about my proposal.

"Do you think there's any point?" he asked.

"Isn't she good enough for him or something?"

"Of course she is, but—" he hesitated, "I'm just not sure it's a very good idea."

"What?"

"Well, I'm not sure they would suit each other."

"Wouldn't it be worth giving it a try?"

He shrugged.

"It's up to you."

The evening was enjoyable but nothing much happened. Shirley Jones flirted constantly with Anthony but he didn't seem to notice. He joked with her as he did with us but when he put his arm around her in a fit of laughter, it was as if he was touching his sister.

The following day Shirley came to me for advice.

"Has he mentioned me at all to you or Jakob?" she asked. I had to admit that he hadn't.

She looked despondent and I felt sorry for her. When she asked me to talk to him and try to get an idea of what he was thinking, I didn't have the heart to refuse.

But nothing ever came of it. The events of the following week saw to that.

I have always tried to do my best. My friends know that I put my all into things, I never shirk or expect more of anyone else than I do of myself. My friends know this and I like to think that our guests at Ditton Hall know it too. Our bookings in recent years testifies to our reputation; it says all that is necessary and so I will refrain from quoting all the newspaper and magazine articles which have been written about us, both in England and abroad. I will just mention the *Daily Telegraph*, *Vogue*, the *Financial Times, Town and Country*, and *Le Monde*. "An oasis in the desert," said the headline in *Town and Country*, for example, and although most of the articles were mainly interested in how we managed to offer international cuisine during a time of isolation and rationing and—I may add— the ignorance of so many English people, there is no question what opinion the writers had of our cooking. Even a child could read between the lines.

Then this fat lump came into my life. This distortion of the flesh. And gave herself airs. As if she had some point to make. As if she knew some secret which is hidden from everyone else—everyone except her!

She arrived on a Friday evening, just before seven. Instead of asking if she could meet me, she plumped straight down in a chair in the dining room and asked for an aperitif. She was fawning about the food as she ate it, no question of that, so the impertinence of her review took me by surprise. When she drove away it was past ten o'clock and the car groaned under her weight.

The article appeared a week later. And the statements, my goodness, the ignorance and pretension! Reading it made me a little sick.

"The salmon is fresh but slightly undercooked for my taste." How did she want it? Like shoe leather? She ate enough of it, anyway; there wasn't a scrap left on the plate when it came back to the kitchen. She must literally have licked it clean, lapped up the sauce with her tongue!

"The duck was tasty but the tiniest bit tough." The only person who would find this duck tough is someone with bad teeth. "Melts in the mouth," said Elizabeth David when she visited us once. And which of them do you suppose is the more reliable? Elizabeth David herself or this monster in human form? This dollop . . . this tub of lard?

"And she didn't even pay," I complained to Anthony. "She ate here free. Imagine!"

"Disa, you didn't want her to pay."

"I won't let people walk all over me like this."

"Don't even think of retaliating. It'll just make bad worse."

"Saying the duck was tough . . ."

"She did praise everything except that and the salmon."

". . . and the salmon undercooked." No, her words wouldn't be allowed to stand.

I sat down in the conservatory and in less than an hour had written a response. Instead of posting it the same day, I took Anthony's advice and slept on it until the following morning. Then I adjusted a word or two but left it largely unchanged.

As time passed I regretted having responded to this dollop. Not, you understand, because I was worried about what I wrote, far from it, I could have been much more pointed. But I should have realized that some people would side with her out of pity.

Certainly some people were shocked when I offered to post her the bones of the duck which she had left behind on the plate. "It won't matter," I wrote, "if the parcel takes a while to arrive as there's not a single morsel of flesh left on the bones." I said I was also prepared to increase the number of dishes on the menu before her next visit as "she obviously went home hungry, having managed to put away only four starters and three main courses. Not to mention dessert, of course." I also promised to invest in wider chairs for the dining room.

When I attended a conference of Restaurateurs de l'Europe in London that autumn, I was surprised that people should still be talking about my article. Some fell silent when I walked by, their eyes shifty like those of children caught in some naughty act, others behaving as if I made them nervous.

"To hell with this rabble," I said to myself. "I have never needed them. To hell with them. I will never be reduced to that."

In the autumn of '38 Jakob became seriously worried about his family in Germany. Admittedly, he had never been one of those who regarded the rise of Nazism as no more than a nasty infection which the country would shake off sooner or later, but even so he didn't realize where it was heading. He made fun of the fact that Aryans were forbidden to work for Jews, saying that no one would listen to such ravings. Frau Hoffman, his parents' housekeeper, disregarded this ban and she was no exception. I suspect now that it was largely his mother's letters which blinded him because she avoided referring to anything unpleasant in them, not wanting to worry him or cause anxiety. "Concentrate on your editorial work, my dear," were the closing words of every letter.

"There's not much news of your father and me. We enjoy God's blessing of being in pretty good health, though your father's prostate bothers him at times. But Dr. Werfel is keeping a close eye on him so he is free from the worst discomfort. Yesterday we had tea with Herr and Frau Krull . . ."

Descriptions of the weather and accounts of trips to concerts, a few words about a book she had read, news of friends.

"Frau Blumenfeld read in an American magazine that our intestines are thirty feet long. I don't know why she told me that . . ."

As the summer passed Jakob began to sense a different tone in the letters. Although she didn't complain about anything and gave no hint that there was anything wrong, it was always as if there were something left unsaid, as if she had made every effort to wield the pen with caution and discipline. Her letters grew shorter but the descriptions of the weather grew longer. She no longer mentioned trips to concerts or parties, and accounts of friends and acquaintances became few and far between.

We weren't the only ones to notice these changes. David, who was starting his studies in London, was no less anxious. He also heard more stories about the situation in Germany than we did and confirmed that everything was not as their mother implied. She didn't even mention the identity cards that Jews were now forced to carry and played down the order that they must not be called by any name except those the authorities ordained. Anna, David's girlfriend, was studying in Holland that winter and he was relieved that she was there rather than in Germany. We didn't miss her. Nor were we ever clear about what exactly she was studying, but for David's sake we didn't ask.

It was in October that Jakob decided to visit his parents. At first both brothers meant to go but eventually Jakob determined that David should stay behind and concentrate on his studies. "There's no need for both of us to go," he said, smiling: "Unless there are some old girlfriends you want to see. And what would Anna have to say about that?"

Jakob booked his flight for early November and let his parents know. His mother did what she could to dissuade him from coming but he stuck to his decision and marked the day on the calendar which hung in the kitchen window. He drew a red ring around the number ten. Under the name of the month, there was a picture of snow falling on fir trees with a round moon hanging over the wood like a paternal eye. Among those trees nothing bad could happen.

We went to London at the beginning of November. Jakob had been offered a position as a teacher at a private school in town and a job was waiting for me with Boulestin, so the time had come to look around for a flat.

Jakob was relieved by this plan. As soon as he had drawn the ring on the calendar he cheered up. Moreover, for the first time in ages we agreed that maybe we should get married while we were in London. I had never told him outright what my mother's reaction had been, but he couldn't help drawing his own conclusions. This time it was I who suggested going to the registry office and I was pleased by how well he received the idea.

Admittedly, we had a quarrel on the way but fortunately I was the one who gave in. There's some consolation in the thought that it was I who made the first gesture of reconciliation.

Jakob had booked a table at Boulestin but didn't tell me until we were on the train to London. He had meant to surprise me. However, I hadn't yet forgiven my patron for his behavior before we moved out to the country and so asked Jakob to cancel the table as soon as we arrived in town. He tried to talk me round but I wouldn't give in. It was then that he lost his temper and spoke sharply to me, probably for the first time. I raised my voice in return but regretted it a few minutes later.

I'm glad I was the one to give in.

When we arrived in London on November 6, the weather was cold and damp, with rain about to turn into snow any minute and a bitter wind. The skies were as gray and chill as the faces of the people in the streets but we tried not to let it affect us. We took a taxi from Paddington and sat in silence during the journey to Camden, where an acquaintance of Jakob's had lent us his flat while he was on a business trip in Manchester. We were relieved when we reached our destination and lit a fire straight away in the sitting room. It warmed up quickly and we lay on the rug in front of the fire to thaw out. When I put my arms around him I forgot the grayness outside, the bitter wind and the cold, forgot everything except what was beautiful and good.

During the next few days we looked around for a flat to rent. We had to force ourselves to go out. All we really wanted to do was to laze about and be with each other. I had begun to dread his absence but naturally didn't mention this to him because I knew it would only make him anxious.

Then, on November 9 we found a flat a short way from Hyde Park, which we both fell in love with. It was small with a balcony at the back and high, narrow windows overlooking the street. There was a tree in front and an empty nest in its branches directly below the sitting room window. The owner was a punctilious little man. We decided to sort out the rental agreement as soon as Jakob returned from Germany in a week's time. The owner wore a hat. I was amused when he doffed it in parting and called me "Madame."

In the evening we dined at Boulestin. There was a big fuss when we appeared in the doorway, and Mrs. Brown flung herself at me, giving me a smacking kiss on the cheek. We sat nearest the kitchen and Boulestin came out and greeted us. I think I can say that my patron and I had buried the hatchet, though we didn't have much to say to each other. One delicacy after another was brought to our table and later, when most of the other diners had left, Mrs. Brown sat down at the piano. We sang and Jakob lit a cigar in honor of eternity, as he expressed it. Yet it was as if some sense of trepidation hung over us. It made itself known when least expected and then Jakob's expression would become distant, until suddenly he came to himself and put his arm around me.

On the way home we decided to visit the registry office the following morning.

But it was never to be.

Jakob's flight was cancelled. We wandered like ghosts around the flat, the newspapers strewn on the floor by the kitchen table, their headlines screaming at us like vendors on a street corner. I felt as if I were suffocating and opened a window to let in some fresh air. A thrush was singing somewhere in the branches of the tree; the weather had cleared up and in the quiet following the rain its song sounded almost ominous, as if it had received news of something we weren't aware of. A book lay on the bedside table and I picked it up, without looking at it. I don't know what book it was, but when I put it down after a long while, there was a damp hand print on the red spine and my palm was blood red. I was filled with horror, and rushing into the bathroom, washed my hands frantically, scrubbing them with a nail brush until the color was gone. By then my hand was stinging and I had drawn blood in two places.

While we had been enjoying ourselves the evening before, Hitler's bully boys had been rampaging round the cities of Germany, attacking Jews. They destroyed their property, set their homes alight, desecrated their synagogues, beating some and killing others. This night became known as *Kristall-nacht*, the night of crystal, for the streets were littered with broken glass from the Jews' shop windows.

All day long Jakob tried in vain to telephone his parents. He was on pins and needles, ringing incessantly, though he knew he wouldn't succeed. We had no appetite and didn't sleep during the night, two ghosts on the prowl, shadows of shadows in the dying light. David came to us around noon and stayed for the rest of the day. He was weak with fear and wouldn't stir from the chair in the corner, from where he could watch his brother alternately lifting and replacing the telephone receiver.

"Are you going to try again?" he asked each time Jakob picked up the phone. And: "Couldn't you get through?" a few moments later.

This monotonous refrain made me even more nervous and I wished he would get out of the chair, put on his coat and leave. "Are you going to try again? Couldn't you get through?" like the ceaseless whining of a baby. His delicate features, which I had always found likable, now only offended me, suggesting the weakness and egotism of a spoiled child. I restrained myself from speaking my mind but sensed that Jakob understood me.

When he finally got a connection late the following day, David had dropped off and was sleeping curled up in the chair in the corner. It was as if he had put down roots in it. Jakob asked me to wake him but for some reason I decided not to. I said I hadn't been able to bring myself to.

The telephone conversation was spasmodic and long-drawn-out. Their mother said that the book shop had been burned to the ground but the family's other property had been left alone, perhaps due to an oversight. They had been deprived of their shares in the newspaper about a month previously but she didn't want to discuss it. Their home had been spared, she said, and that was the most important thing.

I could hear from Jakob's voice that he thought she was hiding something from him.

"Let me talk to Father," he said.

Silence. I moved nearer the phone and heard that she had begun to sob. When she calmed down she told him that his father had fallen ill the morning after the atrocities. She suspected the shock was responsible for preventing him from being able to pass water. He was bursting, she said, wrenched by spasms of pain but couldn't relieve himself however hard he tried. Shortly after midday they had crept out to the car. She couldn't drive so he was forced to take the wheel. They went to Dr. Werfel's surgery without an appointment. She said she was immediately aware from the expression on the nurse's face that all was not well. Dr. Werfel wasn't available, she said. When would he be available?

"He won't be coming in today."

But they could hear the sound of his voice.

"I must talk to him."

"He's not here. Good day."

"I can hear him!"

"Good day!"

When the nurse made as if to show them to the door, Jakob's mother burst in on Dr. Werfel. He had been speaking on the phone.

"I'll have my license taken away if I treat Jews," he said. "I can't take the risk. I'm a family man. Three children . . ."

He slipped a note into her hand.

"You mustn't tell anyone that I have given you his name."

"Dr. Hermann Hölle" was written on the note along with an address. They walked out. The old man was in a bad state but managed to creep back to the car with the help of his wife. Dusk was falling. The streets were wet and slippery. He drove faster than usual and had difficulty controlling his feet when the pain shot down his legs. Eventually, he lost control of the car, which skidded off the road, crashing into a fence. The windscreen shattered and their hands and faces were cut, though not deeply. The steering wheel had split in half but he managed to get hold of two of the spokes which had broken only halfway down and finally maneuvered the car back up on to the road. The rain fell on them through the windscreen. She wiped the water and blood from his face so that he could see the way. One of the headlights was broken.

He collapsed when they entered Dr. Hermann Hölle's surgery. Dr. Hölle drained off his urine but first made them pay four times more than Dr. Werfel usually took for this operation.

Now the old man was in bed.

"He's taking medicine," she said. "You mustn't worry about us. It's over now. I'm sure things will start to settle down."

Two days later Jakob got a flight to Germany. I tried to make him stay in London but couldn't press him too hard. He was restless, convinced that he could help his parents.

"I have to get them out of the country," he said. "The sooner the better."

I accompanied him to the airport in the cold rain. The chairs in the departure lounge were hard and uncomfortable, there was a reek of wet clothing in the air and a fog on the window panes. We held hands in silence while the wind seized sheets of rain and whipped them like clear plastic across the airfield.

We held hands.

When the rain stopped, I said good-bye to him for the last time.

I'm going to address this to you for my own amusement and to pass the time.

In the smoking room they're betting on when land will be sighted. "To the minute," said the learned Dr. Palsson and went round with his hat so that those who were interested could put in a hundred kronur. I thought of you when some-one said: "What if there's a fog?" At that moment I thought of you, perhaps because I had just caught sight of a Bible in the drawer of the bedside table or maybe just because I have always found you rather a misty figure.

I have set eyes on the devil. And whatever you can say about him, you can't deny that he's enterprising. He definitely doesn't sit with his hands in his lap debating with himself. Doesn't say: "What if I did this, what if I did that?" Doesn't ask: "Should I be sending everything up in flames? Perhaps it would be better to let others see to it. Or wait till tomorrow. Yes, I expect it would be more auspicious to post-pone it until tomorrow."

No, he doesn't shirk his tasks, and the results of his work can be seen every day. War, disease, death and famine; false promises and treachery, envy and deceit. One person is set against another and mankind is forever being divided into factions. We hear whispering in dark corners and know that plots are being hatched. No, his works don't pass anyone by. He is always busy, the fellow downstairs.

But you? What about you? Where are you when you're needed? Why do you hide in the mists then?

Once I would get angry with you. I couldn't understand you and used to look into my own heart, in the blind belief that I was responsible for my own happiness. But gradually my eyes were opened and I began to suspect that your indifference wasn't accidental. Is he a coward? I asked myself, or perhaps he just can't be bothered with the struggle anymore. He makes people live in the hope of salvation, promising them life after death. It wouldn't be bad if I could run Ditton Hall in the same way: serve empty plates, promising the guests that their hunger would be assuaged while they slept.

Do I believe in your existence? Oh, I don't know. No doubt I'd feel better if I could answer unconditionally one way or the other but unfortunately that's not possible. Sometimes I even mix you two together, you and the fellow downstairs. Which of them can be behind this? I sometimes ask myself when leafing through a newspaper and reading about some disaster, but I never find the answer. Then the sun will shine through the window onto my table, onto the mushrooms, blackberries, duck or goose, and the wind will whisper sweet nothings to the poplar outside and my thoughts will fortunately turn to other things.

My thoughts often turn to you when I'm at home in Somerset. There the old landowners are losing out one after another to the unscrupulous nouveaux riches. Many members of the old gentry are the salt of the earth and wouldn't hurt a fly, but in the end have nothing to show for it but their title. And memories of ancient renown. But I don't

have anything against them, quite the contrary, I feel sorry
for them.

My thoughts run on like this while Hallgrimur Palsson
thrusts his hat at his fellow passengers and urges them to take
part in the betting.

"What if there's a fog? What then?"

The voices which vanish with the coming of autumn are cheerful and whisper secrets in the fading light as the dusk begins to hover down by the brook like smoke from burning kindling. We pause with the lily ponds and the hedges behind us, holding hands and listening, for the murmurings are low.

"The rumor about the florist," says Anthony.

I remind him of the silence.

"You know it's untrue."

When I was small the breeze sometimes used to carry the scent of heather and wet wool from the moors. Sometimes the echo of hoofbeats, when I sat out in the field waiting for Father to come home. I imagined I could hear his voice in the sound: "Disa, darling, what have you been up to today?"

As the autumn nights draw close, the voices tend to change. Sometimes I don't like it and try to ignore them, avoiding the passages of the old hall and taking care to shuffle through the fallen leaves so that the rustling will drown their whisperings.

What are you doing here? The earth doesn't recognize

your tread, it forgets the sound of your footsteps as soon as you are gone.

If I stand opposite the wall of the hall and call his name, not even the echo of my voice can be heard. "Jakob," I call, "Jakob," but get only silence in return. The same silence as when I tried to reach him after he had gone. A deathly silence.

Anthony's cousin, Lady Galsworthy, a woman in her sixties, tall and thin with an aquiline nose and hawk eyes, stayed with us for nearly a week before Christmas. It must have been two years ago. "It's time you two tied the knot," she said. "For decency's sake, if nothing else."

She wiped the drip from the tip of her red nose with a white handkerchief. "Good gravy, dear," she said to me. "What a difference it would make if my cook could make such good gravy."

She stayed for nearly a week but it was my good fortune that she got the flu and spent three days in bed. I tried to avoid talking to her as far as possible.

She and Anthony used to go sledding together when they were children visiting their grandfather.

"Do you remember when we fell? And you stood up and said . . ."

"Good gravy, dear. For decency's sake, if nothing else."

"I want you to know it's untrue what they say about us," repeats Anthony. "I hardly know the man."

We stroll home. I can't stand this weakness and am ready to explode at him when suddenly I hear a cheerful voice in the breeze and bite my tongue. I'm convinced it's a child's voice, a boy laughing. Perhaps he's with his mother down by the road.

"Untrue," he says.

Over the fields the blue dusk rolls like slow waves toward a deserted shore.

We will reach Iceland at nine tomorrow morning. I receive the news with mixed feelings, glad to be free of this deadly dull company but nervous about my homecoming.

What do I have to say to him? My words can never be anything but an epilogue. They cannot help him in any way. What can he know about me? What can he want to know about me? As little as possible, I imagine.

Why are you doing this? I ask myself, listening to the autumn rain beating on the porthole. Why? I need fresh air.

Someone says he saw two gulls flying by a moment ago. I go up on deck and think I see a white wing in the mist, a white wing which turns into a speck of light and vanishes. I have a premonition of a rock out in the fog, a rock covered with seaweed and a seal clambering on to it. Why, I don't know. My thoughts are wandering. I try but cannot control them.

The clowns await the evening in their best clothes, newly shaven and reeking of aftershave, wet-combed, with an aperitif in their hands, smiling and happy as slugs in damp moss. They're free of all doubt and anxiety, adjusting their ties for the fourth time, looking in the mirror and watching themselves raising their drinks to their lips.

The women are doubtless still powdering their noses, as special care must be taken in all the preparations for the final dinner. Tomorrow they will be back in their gray, mundane lives, half-dried haddock and boiled potatoes, children crying in the night and emptiness by day, a furtive glass of sherry in the evening to try to dispel the gloom. The wheels keep turning and the bells conscientiously mark each step toward the end. Sometimes someone gets a promotion and a party is thrown. "Head accountant," says the wife to her friends and looks with admiring eyes at her husband who puts on a modest face, though he knows he deserves the position. All that drudgery for all those years.

There's a poker game in progress in the smoking room when I come in again. The learned doctor is in full flight, the first glass having lifted his soul from the depths of his hangover. Apparently he remembers our last exchange and takes care to avoid my eye.

"Good evening, Madam!" cries his companion. "Can we invite you to join us for a hand?"

My thoughts turn to Anthony.

That spring we had decided to repair the stone wall down by the road, as well as the wall between the main building and the conservatory. It was also a matter of urgency to wallpaper and paint the guest rooms in the north wing, though perhaps it could be claimed that it was no less a priority to carpet the billiards room and games room. Then Anthony pointed out that it would be better to replace the netting around the tennis courts sooner rather than later, and I didn't see how we could delay any longer putting new glass in the greenhouse. On top of all this came the traditional spring chores which Old Marshall usually took care of. Only this time we couldn't rely on him because he had fallen when climbing down from the tractor a week before, slipping on wet wood and breaking his leg.

"He'll have to start cutting down anyway," I told Anthony. "The dear chap is getting old, as you know."

Anthony tried to cut such talk short. "That sort of mishap could happen to anyone," I remember him muttering.

I then said something along the lines that perhaps someone else could take care of the heaviest jobs.

"You can be the one to tell him," he replied.

Of course, neither of us could summon the courage to discuss this with the old man. It's not as if we didn't have other things to attend to, with no more than a month left till the first guests were expected. We had often been let down by the firm of workmen we had used during the past few seasons— they were extortionately expensive—and so we decided to let things take their course and advertise for handymen to help us.

Having carefully scrutinized all the offers we received, we agreed to hire two men from Surrey. What decided the matter was that they claimed to have worked for Lord Greene of Joldwynd.

"The people at Joldwynd should know about workmen after all the bother they've had there," said Anthony. "Only seven years after his house was built, Lord Greene was advised to knock it down and build a new one from scratch. An excellent fellow, Lord Greene," he added.

I asked him to speak to Lord Greene to check up on the men's reliability but for some reason he never got round to it.

For the first week they never stopped working. They slept in the east wing and were up with the lark, worked all day, didn't linger over their meals but ate in silence in the kitchen and went early to bed. They were both in their late thirties, one lean and slight in appearance, the other burly but not tall. They began outside, as it was fairly mild and dry for the first few days. The stones which had fallen out of the wall by the conservatory were back in place in no time and the wall by the entrance was soon as good as new. The day they began to put up new netting around the tennis courts it started to rain and I expected them to take a break from outdoor tasks and come inside. But they kept going, putting on mackintoshes and boots, and not letting the downpour interfere with their work. I breathed more easily and told Anthony that I didn't know how we had ever managed without them.

The painting went without a hitch but by then their meal breaks seemed to be getting longer. They also went to bed later than before, generally sitting in the billiards room in the evenings, playing cards, sometimes rummy but more often poker. I suspected them of playing for money.

Anthony sometimes looked in on them in the evenings and in my opinion the burlier man was rather too matey with him, so I tried to make sure that his visits to them didn't last long. Eventually I had to tell him that I thought it best if he stayed away from them completely in the evenings.

When they had been with us for just under three weeks, I had to go on a brief trip. I went away every year at this time, taking little Marilyn with me and traveling for two to three days. We didn't go far, no farther than Hampshire or Devon, sometimes to Wiltshire and a couple of times to Cornwall. This trip was undertaken in search of good fresh ingredients at reasonable prices and we visited one farm after another, often four or five in the same day. Of course, I have always been loyal to the Wakefields, but there's no harm in having other cards up my sleeve when it comes to negotiating with them. In addition, I must admit that not everything they provide is equally good. For example, I have made it my custom to buy duck and pheasant from Liphook in Hampshire and make sure I have the papers lying on the table when Mr. Wakefield comes to do a deal with me. "The Liphook Game Farm," meets his eye, "Supplies Pheasant Eggs from a Stock of 10,000 Birds. Cross Mongolian Eggs at Reasonable Prices (I underline 'reasonable' in red so it definitely won't escape his attention), All Infertile Eggs Replaced. Wild Ducks for your Pleasure, etc."

We hadn't got farther than the outskirts of Salisbury when I was struck with a sense of unease. The spire of the cathedral

appeared above the woods ahead of us against the backdrop
of a few aimlessly drifting clouds, humble as an index finger
reaching out to the Almighty and usually a comforting sight.
As it rose before me, I felt nervous, though I gave no sign of
it, either in the car or later when we stopped at a pig farm
and stepped out into the mild air. We looked around quickly
as usual, but I felt worse and worse as day wore on. We had
planned to eat supper with the people at Liphook and stay
there overnight, but when the meal was over and we sat
down in the sitting room with a cup of coffee and glass of
port, I suddenly decided to go home. Perhaps Marilyn had
already sensed that something was wrong. She asked no
questions, just gathered our things together and roused the
driver, who had probably been dropping off.

A mist shrouded the landscape on the way home and from
time to time the heavens opened. When we stopped at a narrow bridge over the Avon, I opened the window and thought
I could hear an owl hooting in the darkness. In the distance
the clouds gleamed.

When we drew up at the house, it was past one o'clock.
Lights blazed from many of the windows in the main block
and I smelled woodsmoke as soon as I opened the car door.
The chimney was pouring out smoke and the front door
stood wide open. I walked straight in and didn't stop until I
came to the door of the billiards room. The first person I saw
was our neighbor, the Earl of Helmsdale, who had nodded
off in a chair by the fire. Then, as I got nearer, I caught sight
of Anthony and the workmen. Anthony tried to focus on
me with bleary eyes. He was dead drunk, sitting or rather
slumped at the card table, too far gone to open his mouth.
The workmen sat there with him, also drunk but still with
their wits about them.

"Welcome, madam," said the burly man.

"Welcome to our house," said the other. "Next time perhaps you wouldn't mind knocking before you enter."

"And wiping your shoes."

They laughed like madmen.

Empty bottles lay littered across the floor: whiskey, gin, and two red wine bottles, a 1951 Margaux and a '45 Mouton which I had put by as an investment. The Earl of Helmsdale snored, while Anthony took off his hunting cap and stared at it as if he had never seen it before.

"Our mate Anthony put the house up in the last game," said the burly man.

"We've got the paper to prove it," added the other, waving a sheet of pale yellow stationery at me which I recognized at once. It was my writing paper. They couldn't have got hold of it from anywhere but the desk in my bedroom.

"How dare you!"

"We'll employ you in the kitchen. Someone's got to feed us."

"And wash up. Someone's got to wash up too."

"You will regret this!"

"Anthony, wake up! Wake up, mate! Tell us about this florist we've been hearing about."

At that point I lost my temper. Before I knew it I was down in the cellar, flinging open the door of the gun store. I seized a Browning double-barreled shotgun, loaded it in a tearing hurry and raced up the stairs. Marilyn was just coming in with our things.

"Disa? What's going on?"

Without answering her I stormed into the billiards room, not stopping till I got to the card table and aimed the shotgun first at the burly man, then at his companion.

"Get out!"

They were stunned, either with amazement or fright, and

didn't move. But having reached the end of my tether, I took aim at the hearth and fired. The shot reverberated through the house, whining up the chimney and waking the birds in the trees, rousing the ghosts in the attics and echoing in the quiet of the night. The two men leaped to their feet and dashed to the door in a panic. I followed close on their heels as they ran away from the house, firing again when I thought they were slowing down.

"Did you get the lion?" bellowed the Earl of Helmsdale when I returned.

I advised him to go back to sleep.

The next day I had the driver track down the men in the village. He took all their gear with him and a check for what we owed them. Though in fact I amused myself by subtracting the price of the bottle of Mouton which they had been so bold as to pilfer from me. I can confidently say that never before or since have they had to pay so much for a drink.

The Radstock police station is a poky little building beside the library. There is a small sign above the door and from a distance the picture looks like the spring and cogs of a clock mechanism. Those who approach closer will see, however, that the spring is the remains of a bouquet of flowers and the cogs are what is left of the "s" in Est. and the eights in 1888. Few people now remember that there was once a florist in this house but it has never occurred to the policemen to take down the sign. After all, their job is generally quiet: there's little traffic and the townspeople are a peaceable lot, so it is perfectly appropriate—on most days—to receive visitors beneath a faded picture of flowers.

So it wasn't surprising that they were wholly unprepared for the incident which I intend to recount here—indeed they were exceedingly relieved when Jakob and I appeared at the reception desk.

Anthony had sent a message to Jakob that morning asking him to come and meet him as quickly as he could get down to the police station. I joined him. We cycled as fast as we could but when we were almost there, I got a puncture in my front tire. I told Jakob to go on without me, pushed my bike into the town and went to get the puncture mended before trudging over to the police station. The day was overcast with a chilly breeze but I was sweaty from the cycle ride and not warmly dressed. I felt a chill.

Jakob was with Anthony and two policemen in a room off the reception area. The door was shut. The sergeant behind the desk was clearly very uncomfortable, fidgeting and repeating at regular intervals: "I'm sure there must be some mistake." Then he looked at the clock on the wall and added: "They should be out soon."

The clock ticked and from time to time somebody would pass and nod through the window or touch the brim of his hat. Otherwise, nothing happened until Jakob opened the door and beckoned me to come outside with him. Anthony remained sitting at a table in the room. He was deathly pale but still tried to give me a smile. He looked as if he had been crying.

"Someone is threatening to charge Anthony with indecent behavior," explained Jakob when we were out in the street. "The father of some young man whom Anthony is supposed to have had a relationship with."

"What?" I exclaimed.

"Slept with, Disa. He could get into a lot of trouble."

At first I was completely bewildered but gradually the meaning filtered through to me.

Anthony had asked Jakob to talk to the young man's father and try to come to an arrangement. The police didn't know which way to turn and found this state of affairs extremely embarrassing.

"I'm going to meet the old man later today," Jakob told me. "It should be interesting."

The boy's father turned out to be nothing more than a common thug who had threatened Anthony to extort money from him. The son sat at a distance while his father and Jakob argued, standing up every now and then when his father saw fit to hurl abuse at him or threaten him. The young man, who couldn't have been more than about twenty, listened in silence but Jakob thought his eyes looked sly.

Naturally, the man's demands were outrageous but after Jakob had twice stood up and threatened to walk out, they finally came to an agreement. According to this, father and son should receive one lump sum, a quarter of what the old man had originally demanded, and in return sign a statement to the effect that relations between Anthony and the young man had not been in any way immoral, so that the father and son would not dream of pressing charges against Mr. Anthony Lonsdale either then or at a later date.

Anthony wept when we handed over the signed statement. We were glad to have been of service to him, despite the disagreeable nature of the affair. However, I thought it best not to bother trying to sound him out on the subject of Miss Shirley Jones.

"In the sight of your Maker," as Mother was in the habit of saying to us children when we did something to displease her. "Disa, don't use such language. You sully your soul in the sight of your Maker. What behavior, children. What a way to behave in the sight of your Maker."

That gaze never seemed far away when I was a child. Sometimes it dogged my heels or lay in wait, ever ready to be shocked by me. Or rather: ever hoping I would offend it.

When I was in my teens I began to regard it as arrogant and haughty, proud and even prudish. I sometimes saw its owner in my mind: an old man sitting on a bench throwing bread-crumbs to pigeons and starlings, taking offense when the birds fought over the crumbs at his feet.

As the years passed I thought of that gaze less often. I didn't think much about death or the end either because I was carefree, both when Jorunn and I lived in Reykjavik and later when I sailed to England. Then the gaze of my Maker left me in peace, as did his justice—his justice which is nothing but punishment, his love which is nothing but contempt, his touch which is a blow, his mercy which is death. Then my

Maker left me in peace and threw his breadcrumbs to other small birds, contentedly watching them at his feet. The days were bright and the nights warm as a cloak mantling the soul. No one reprimanded me and there was no shadow of a premonition on my mind.

"Mors est quies viatoris," his clowns whisper to us, death is rest to the traveler. "Pie Iesu domine dona eis requiem." Merciful Lord Jesus, grant them rest. Anthony weeps when he repeats these words in your church because he knows that he is not pleasing in your eyes. "Mors est quies," but after life there is nothing, though your charlatans never tire of their salesmanship, forever tempting the gullible with the promise of eternity.

And so I was free from your kiss which burns and your sheltering hand which is always ready to strike, and so I was free until the day I rang Mother and told her that Jakob and I were engaged. That night your gaze chased me from dream to dream, accusatory, vengeful.

When I woke with a jolt in the middle of the night, weak with emotion, it stared into my face. I met the look and suddenly recognized it. In an instant the veil was stripped away. It was the gaze of my mother. That was what had pursued me all those years.

Self-pity doesn't help anyone, nothing can be undone, nothing changed. The candle burns and its flame, slender and feeble, gropes for a purchase in the darkness before guttering and dying. We guess what lies behind the door but ask no questions. We take delight in a sunbeam on a windowpane and fear the night. Fate, we say, instead of looking into our own hearts.

I took a painkiller half an hour ago which is making it difficult to concentrate. My fingers are cramped round the medicine bottle but slide apart without my being able to control them. I can see the book *Help Yourself;* I know it's this book, even though it's a blur and I can't read the letters.

In Bath, just by the Pulteney Bridge over the Avon, there was a little quay hung with pretty lanterns. There were also seats beside the lanterns where one could rest one's tired legs; I remember that older people in particular used to sit there, people who had retired and perhaps had nothing else to do but watch the river flowing by. But I also have an impression of young people walking hand in hand along the quayside in the twilight, putting their heads together and whispering to one another. The young people didn't mind when it rained, seeming when the first drops fell to enjoy the dash for cover under the leafy canopy of trees in the park.

After David had received confirmation that Jakob and his parents were in Buchenwald, I went alone to Somerset to fetch my belongings. They weren't anything special, just clothes and books, and fitted easily into a couple of medium-sized suitcases. I left the rest behind so that Jakob and I could return for it later.

Anthony joined me in the evening and we went to Bath together just as the lamps were being lit. There were fewer people than usual down by the river, as there was a nippy wind coming off the water and the awnings hung forlornly over the seats, while the light from the lanterns didn't seem as comforting as before. Anthony tried again to make me change my mind about going home to Iceland.

"You can live with me," he said. "There's enough room, after all. It won't be long before he comes back."

But his words were only wishful thinking, and the wind snatched them from his lips and blew them away before I was ready to answer. He knew I couldn't stay there any longer. Everything reminded me of Jakob.

"Without him . . ." I began, but couldn't finish the sentence.

"You know you're always welcome."

"I'll come when they let him go. Until then, I'll stay in Iceland."

"Then you'll both come."

"Then we'll both come."

The train to London rattled along as if nothing had happened, hooting now and then in the night as if to leave behind a memorial to something that would never return. I was too tired to sleep, too listless to feel any pain. Why did I let him go? Why didn't I beg him to stay?

Fortunately, the train was nearly empty but I can still remember my compartment after all these years. Every tiny detail is engraved on my mind. I can even see the split seam in the seat in front of me, running right across the seat so that the stuffing bulged out in the middle. The seat was red.

When we arrived in London it was snowing. I was caught unprepared.

Did I expect to see him again? I don't know, can't work out when I gave up hope, don't know whether I ever really succeeded in deceiving myself completely.

All people knew about Buchenwald then was that it was a prison camp. The truth about concentration camps came later. When I tried to imagine the prison camp I generally saw Jakob doing hard labor and convinced myself that he would be able to bear it as he was strong and healthy, both mentally and physically. Gradually, however, this image faded as rumors began to circulate, each more horrific than the last. But by then I was in Iceland and there is no point recalling them now when they are common knowledge.

We had a bad crossing home on the *Bruarfoss* and I spent most of the voyage lying below deck, throwing up. I kept seeing Jakob before me as he looked when we said good-bye at the airport. In my delirium he would sometimes change into a shadow and then I would jolt upright with the reek of wet clothing in my nostrils and a fog before my eyes. Father had promised to come to Reykjavik to meet me and I tried not to think of anything but his embrace and the smile of my sister

Joka whom I had missed so much. From time to time I must have been delirious because the captain later said that he had been worried about me. On second thought, I believe the delirium did me good, deadening the suffering and making time pass more quickly.

I was bed-bound for a week after my homecoming. It was comforting staying with my sister Joka and her husband, Gunnar, and the chirping of Helga, their three-month-old daughter, cheered me up. Father spent the first days with me but then he had to go back up north to see his patients. Before he said good-bye, he arranged a job for me at number 56 Fjolugata with Bolli Haraldsson, the bank manager, and his wife, Gudrun. Gudrun was an invalid, he said, she suffered from depression which had grown worse since their son went abroad.

"She must be pretty frail," he said. "They need a cook."

"Will I be living in?"

"Just while you're getting back into shape, Disa dear. Later you can always get a job with Sivertsen at Hotel Borg. When you feel up to it."

He didn't know Dr. Bolli himself but Vilhjalmur Borg spoke well of him, he said.

When I was back on my feet, I took up the habit of smoking cigarillos for comfort. I went for daily walks to regain my strength, sometimes to Mrs. Olsen, but more often down to the harbor to gaze out to sea. Most days were gray but once or twice the wintry sun shone in a cloudless sky and it was possible to look forward to seeing the moon in the evening. Cigarillos, ten to a packet. I restricted myself to smoking no more than five a day to give myself something to look forward to.

After a month had passed, I rang Father and told him that I was ready to start work. By the following day he had given notice of my arrival at number 56 Fjolugata.

Now we are sailing the waves which I used to gaze at from the harbor in the old days, when I would smoke cigarillos and blow the smoke out into the indifferent breeze. Mount Esja is drawing near and so are the cathedral, the Catholic church on the hill and the warehouses down by the harbor. I have a premonition of the smell of tar and sacking as we draw closer. The gulls soar around the ship as if they have received some secret intelligence of a catch. They have the sense to keep quiet about it.

My fellow passengers are mostly under the weather following last night's revelry. A young man, who claims to be a great singer, won the bet despite the fact that fog hid the land from sight all night. At some time during the first watch he claimed that he could smell Iceland and the captain confirmed that land would have been sighted a few minutes earlier if there hadn't been a fog. Hallgrimur Palsson celebrated. The singer belted out "Oh blessed art thou summer sun" and offered those still standing whiskey and gin. I slipped away to my cabin, climbed into bed and turned my face to the wall.

But now no one is singing; they are red of eye and pale of

cheek. A man from first class who has been sleeping with a girl from second class for the whole trip, now pretends he doesn't know her, as his wife is waiting for him on the docks with their two daughters. They are all wearing red hats and wave to the ship as we approach. He is a bit sheepish as he waves back. And the learned Dr. Palsson is silent at last as he greets his parents. Perhaps he now regrets not having taken my advice.

I take a taxi to Hotel Borg where I intend to stay while I'm in Iceland.

"Asdis Jonsdottir," says the girl at reception. "Six nights."

When I open the door to my room I feel an indescribable emptiness.

Later I couldn't remember whether it was the bowl of apples I noticed first or the shaft of sunlight falling on them between the thick curtains. I hadn't seen such beautiful apples since leaving England, red and shiny like precious gems. I yearned to touch them and moved closer to the table where the bowl stood on a round, yellow cloth but stopped at the last moment and made do with reaching out my hand and grasping at the sunbeam. A shadow fell on the apples in the dim drawing room and I instantly whipped back my hand in order to see them shine anew.

It was then that a voice spoke behind me: "They'll rot too, if they're forgotten."

I wasn't startled because the voice was gentle and amiable. He took off his glasses and wiped them with a handkerchief, inspecting them absentmindedly, then instead of putting them back on, twisted them between his fingers, clockwise and counterclockwise in turn.

"It's getting dark," he said eventually and switched on the lamp beside the bowl. "These long, dark winter nights."

I was about to point out that it would still be light if he

were to draw back the heavy curtains, but thought better of it.

"I woke to the snow buntings this morning," he continued. "They had found some treat in the garden after last night's rain. I enjoy watching them, so I went out on to the balcony in the dawn breeze to get a better view. Poor things," he said finally, then fell silent, putting an end to these ramblings. He invited me to sit down but remained standing himself, rubbing his glasses with the handkerchief while pacing up and down, obviously out of habit.

"The winter has a bad effect on my wife. Apart from the Advent season, of course, when she always takes part in the Christmas preparations. Rushes round the house, making sure all the rooms are decorated, and lighting candles from dawn to dusk. She does her bit when it comes to baking and making leaf-bread too and the house is filled with the smell day after day. With a smile on her lips, my dear, a smile on her lips."

He fell silent before adding: "But now Christmas is over. And some people find the winter months slow to pass."

He was stocky without being precisely fat, jollier than in the photographs in the newspapers. His eyes were shrewd but at the same time distant, his hair gray at the temples and his hands more delicate than his build would suggest.

"You had better know straightaway that my wife rarely leaves her room in the winter. On bad days she stays in bed but when she's feeling better she sits by the doors to the balcony, which has a view over the bay. She's from the west of the country. She likes to watch the sea. You should know all about that," he added with a smile, "a girl from Kopasker."

I nodded and muttered something about understanding what he meant.

"We have to make sure that she eats, as generally she doesn't have much appetite. The maid does what she can but she only knows the absolute basics. I'm hoping that better food will help restore her health. In fact, I'm sure it will."

He fell silent and inspected the reflection in his glasses; it was as if he didn't quite know how to finish his description of life in the household. Just as it looked as if he was about to continue, a voice called down from upstairs.

"Bolli! Come here! Oh, Bolli . . ." The voice lifted on the final syllable.

He started, then without seeming unduly agitated asked me to excuse him and went out. I heard his slow, even tread going up the stairs to the first floor where he knocked lightly on a door before opening it and saying, "My dear . . ."

I glanced round at the heavy furniture, a sofa covered with red velvet and two chairs belonging to the same set, a mahogany table and vase of flowers, a stuffed eagle and a painting of a woman holding a book. She was delicate and pretty but I sensed the sadness in her eyes. Just as I was walking over to the picture, a girl entered the room. Small, brisk, no more than about twenty.

"That's the mistress," she said, adding in explanation, "in the picture. When she was young."

Then she introduced herself as Maria, the family maid.

"My name's Asdis. How do you do?"

She inspected me for a moment, then darted to the mahogany table and seized a half-empty glass of sherry which had been left on top of a magazine.

"He'll never finish this," she said as if to herself. "It's been here since yesterday evening."

She wiped the dust off the table with the corner of her apron, then said good-bye, wishing me luck.

Outside, the sun went behind a cloud and a shadow settled on the bowl of apples, despite the lamp on the table beside it. It was as if the glow was absorbed by the bowl without illuminating it. The gleam disappeared from the apples and I almost took the fact to heart. Then the clouds parted again and the late afternoon sun darted between the curtains, bathing the apples and my mood with light.

"It doesn't take much either way," I said to myself.

Shortly afterward Dr. Bolli came downstairs. This time he made sure that the drawing room door closed properly behind him.

"Once I had a meeting with some men who were complete strangers to me," he began. "But when I sat down at my desk opposite them, I felt as if I had met them all before. I felt as if I had sat opposite them at the same desk, in the same chair, at the same time of day to discuss the same things. I even imagined I had heard them utter the same words and seen them make the same movements. Suddenly, I had a premonition that one of them had a gold front tooth. He had sat in silence until then and I became impatient to see him open his mouth. I remembered a joke I had recently read in *Icelandic Humor* and decided to repeat it, though I don't usually make jokes while I'm working. He smiled at first without revealing his teeth, then roared with laughter along with the others and the gold glittered in his mouth. I thought I was going mad and spent the rest of the meeting in a state. Later I remembered what my dear old grandmother used to say when I was a boy: The mind of man is a great labyrinth. Oh yes, so it is. And it is easier to judge others than to know oneself."

There was a sound of voices outside the room. He listened but remained where he was. After a moment, there was a knock at the door and Maria popped in her head without waiting for an answer.

"The Minister's here," she announced. "He's waiting in the study."

"Take him some coffee, would you? I'll be along in a moment."

"Well, Asdis."

"Is there anything you'd like to know about me, sir? You haven't asked me anything."

He smiled.

"No need for titles. We're not so formal in this household. I know all I need to know. Vilhjalmur told you about the wages and conditions, didn't he?"

I nodded.

"If you'd like the job . . ."

"I'd be very grateful."

". . . then Maria will show you your room and all the nooks and crannies in the kitchen. Your room catches the sun in the mornings and so does the kitchen. Even in the autumn. You can start on Monday . . . unless it would suit you better to begin earlier. Superstition, you see . . . But it's up to you."

"It would suit me to start on Monday," I replied.

He held out his hand to me and I stood up to shake it. Then he was gone.

When I emerged on to the street it had begun to snow. The wind had also blown up and whirled the snow around my legs. A little way from the house I looked back over my shoulder. In a window on the top floor I glimpsed a face watching me. It was as white as the snow and vanished as soon as my eye fell on it.

The snow covered my tracks on the pavement.

I didn't see the mistress of the house for the first three weeks. Maria arrived in the mornings and left in the evenings, sometimes late if Dr. Bolli had guests. She also had a little attic room for her use if she chose to stay over, but this rarely happened as the room was inadequately heated. She delivered messages to me from the mistress, usually verbally but occasionally in little notes. The mistress had elegant handwriting. The messages were mostly about cooking. She asked me, for example, to get in touch with two ship's captains who she knew could get hold of goods unavailable in the shops, and a Dane who lived in Hafnarfjordur and provided the Danish embassy with various luxuries. I noticed that her appetite grew from day to day; sometimes her plates would come back empty on good days, usually when the sun was out. Then she would also put records on the gramophone in her room, generally Mozart or Verdi. "La Forza del Destino" was a particular favorite. Maria said that she had praised the food and was looking forward to meeting me but wasn't quite ready yet. I didn't ask any questions.

The little blue mirror by the cooker became my friend right away, though sometimes I saw things reflected in it which I didn't want to see. There were times when I thought I saw myself through someone else's eyes when I looked into it, someone who was fond of me and was thinking of me. Then I would also sense the nearness of the pond in the woods where Jakob and I used to splash around, see our faces reflected in the rainwater that had collected during the night in the old wheel-ruts leading to our cottage. Sometimes steam rose from the earth early in the morning as if it were breathing. Sometimes the earth spoke to us.

Perhaps it was the handpainted flowers on the frame which had this effect on me, at least they always reminded me of things I found beautiful and kind. Sometimes I've thought of asking some handy carpenter to make me the same kind of frame and paint it according to my instructions, but I haven't yet dared.

One Saturday, shortly after midday, the mistress finally sent for me.

"She's waiting," said Maria, "so you'd better hurry."

I'd known something was up, as Maria had been running around her all morning, from the moment she woke at ten. This was unusually early; in fact, often she didn't stir till noon. I suspect sleeping pills played their part in this. I glanced in the mirror, brushed a lock of hair from my forehead, then took off my apron and hurried upstairs.

The mistress sat in a chair by the balcony doors, looking out. She wore a red silk dress, a pearl necklace and a bracelet on her left arm as if she were going to a party. Maria had combed and arranged her hair, which was brown with chestnut lights in it. A faint scent of grass lingered in the room. She invited me to sit down beside her, indicating with her head toward the window.

"The sea looks beautiful today," she said.

Then she reached out to the gramophone beside her and put on a record.

"Listen," she said.

"Pace, pace," sang Leonora, *"mio Dio, pace, mio Dio."*

We sat still, gazing out of the window. A flock of thrushes flew by. Clouds appeared on the horizon. We looked out of the window in silence.

"Pace, pace . . ."

She shifted in her chair, closed her eyes and took my hand. We sat like this until the needle lifted from the record and silence enfolded us. I didn't find it at all uncomfortable; warmth and sincerity emanated from her hand. And fear.

She drew back her hand and rose slowly to her feet. When I took hold of the door handle on my way out, she said, "Our son is in Germany. I know how you feel."

I took a long time descending the stairs.

I had neither written to my mother nor spoken to her on the phone since I came home. Nor had I received a letter from her. Father and Jorunn did what they could to bring about a reconciliation, Father in his quiet way, Jorunn more insistently whenever we were alone together. But I couldn't forgive Mother, however hard I tried, and asked Jorunn to change the subject, reminding her that Mother hadn't even offered me a helping hand when Jakob was put in the prison camp. Hadn't bothered to come to Reykjavik to meet me. Hadn't picked up the phone to comfort me. Hadn't even put pen to paper. She had behaved as if I weren't her concern, as I said to Jorunn, and I wasn't about to please her by seeking her good opinion. An error in the bookkeeping, I told Jorunn. That's all I am to her.

Yet as the spring wore on, I found myself compelled to sit at the desk in my room at 56 Fjolugata and try to put down on paper my thoughts about our relationship. I had half a mind to send them to her in a letter if I was satisfied with the result but for a long time it didn't look as if I would ever manage to come to a conclusion. Yet somehow the letter grew line by line until early one Saturday I faced the fact that I was ready to finish it. Although a long time has passed and I haven't taken the letter out of my desk for many years, it sticks in my memory how fair and just I tried to be in those pages which ran to five sheets by the time I had finished. For some reason I thought it was sensible not to sign the letter until the following day, letting it wait overnight in case it occurred to me to change something or cross something else out. I put the sheets in my desk drawer along with the envelope which I hadn't yet addressed, put on my coat and went out. Jorunn had been ill and we hadn't met for a week or so, but she had never left my thoughts while I was writing to Mother. I decided to wander over to see her and her husband, but first I wanted to feed the ducks on the pond with a few stale breadcrumbs from the kitchen.

It was a damp, chilly day, though it had begun promisingly with pale sunshine and a gentle breeze in the trees. But now it was trying to rain and the wind howled like a beaten dog, as it fumbled for dead leaves to sweep up off the pavements. The lights in the windows of the houses looked cheerless and feeble. It was impossible to prevent the grayness from seeping in through my eyes and settling over my thoughts. I was trying to drive it away when I suddenly witnessed an odd incident down on Laekjargata. It remained fixed in my memory, but I wouldn't record it here were it not for the fact that the person responsible for the incident was present at a later date, when the veil of deception was lifted from my eyes.

There was no one about apart from me and an old man who sat on a bench in front of the old theater, staring into space. Maybe he was holding a bag of bread, maybe not.

A swan took off from the lake. I noticed it immediately as its flight was uneven and clumsy as if it were wounded and couldn't use one of its wings properly. It didn't get very high and quickly lost momentum until finally it crashed on to the road. I wasn't far off and began to run but slowed down when a car approached and stopped in front of the bird. The driver got out. I recognized both him and the car, as his boss was a frequent visitor at 56 Fjolugata: Hallur Steinsson, editor and importer. The swan lay in the road, jerking from time to time, struggling to get on its feet. The chauffeur hesitated in the middle of the road, moved a step closer to the bird and inspected it, then stepped back and stood looking stumped. At that moment, the rear door of the car opened and Hallur Steinsson heaved himself out of his seat and stretched his legs out on to the road. This maneuvre wasn't achieved without effort as he was clearly drunk.

"Can't we get a move on?"

"I'm not driving over the bird."

"Isn't it dead?"

"No, it's alive."

"Well, shove it out of the way. We haven't got all day."

A young woman clambered out of the car behind him, hobbled over to the chauffeur on her high heels and steadied herself against him. I had seen Hallur Steinsson's wife more than once, but she was probably at home doing her embroidery when this incident took place. Or baking doughnuts. Or perhaps at a meeting of the women's institute. Anyway, the editor and importer told the girl to get back into the car and keep out of sight, but she ignored his orders.

"Poor thing," she said. "It's crying. Can't you see it's crying?"

Hallur Steinsson had had enough.

"Get rid of the blasted creature, I say! Right now!"

When the chauffeur didn't immediately react, his boss got to work himself. He strode purposefully over to the bird, grabbed it around the neck and dragged it to the gutter. The girl exclaimed "Jesus!" but the chauffeur looked away. Perhaps the editor and importer momentarily imagined himself a big game hunter, for he smiled triumphantly as if he had brought down a whopper. But his smile quickly disappeared when the swan twisted round and closed its beak on his buttock. He let out a yell of pain and tried to shake off the bird, striking out at it and lurching toward the car, screaming at the chauffeur to "do something," only ceasing his cries when the bird gave up and collapsed back on to the road, this time with a torn shred of trouser in its beak.

The boss jumped behind the steering wheel and ordered both girl and chauffeur into the back. As he stormed off down the road I noticed that the rear door had slammed on the girl's dress, leaving the skirt hanging out.

The dress was red and flapped in the biting winter wind.

Jorunn had gone out. Her husband, Gunnar, rose from the green chair by the window when I came in and then returned to it. He'd been reading a book. Behind him I could see the gray snowdrifts on the slopes of Mount Esja, gray sky and gray sea. Little Helga was asleep.

"She's gone out to the shop," he explained. "She'll be back in a minute."

He looked at the clock.

"She should be back already. I've got a late shift."

I told him to get along, as it didn't take two of us to look after the child.

"I've got nothing better to do," I added.

He was a quiet, reliable and likable man, though not particularly jolly. I always liked him. When Jorunn died he blamed himself.

So I was glad when I heard a few years ago that he had taken up with a woman, though admittedly I know nothing about her. I have a feeling she's a teacher or works at a kindergarten, though I couldn't swear.

Helga slept peacefully, her face faintly lit by a small lamp on the windowsill. She was like her mother; I wonder if she still is? I'd like to meet her while I'm here.

The flat was small but neat, not a speck of dust and everything in its proper place. Jorunn had arranged knick-knacks here and there for decoration and pleasure; ornaments and pebbles, two red boxes I'd sent her from England, an old alarm clock of Grandmother's which no longer worked, a silver inkstand and quill pen, and a white wagtail's egg which we had found on the moors down by the stream when we were small and which Father had ordered us to put on display in our bedroom as a permanent reminder of how naughty we had been. On a round table in the sitting room were a small blue cloth and a vase of dried flowers, a book of poems and a few letters which Jorunn had bound together with yellow ribbon. I went over and picked up the letters after a moment's thought. I recognized the writing on the top envelope: they were from Mother.

That morning I had put on the necklace which Jakob bought for me in Bath as a birthday present and I now began unconsciously to fiddle with it. A tremor ran through the peace in the room and I put down the letters for a second while I recovered my composure, then reached out for them again, hesitantly, to be sure, and undid the ribbon. Mrs. Jorunn Jonsdottir, 24 Frakkastigur, Reykjavik. Two twenty-aurar stamps, a red *Gullfoss.* The letter on the top of the pile was postmarked two weeks ago. I opened the envelope.

Fate, people call it, instead of looking into their own hearts . . . I would have been much happier if I had never read that letter. Or put it in my pocket before leaving. Kept it with me ever after. And read it again and again to confirm that I had been in the right and my behavior afterward had been justifiable. Fate, people call it; I can't help laughing.

. . . I have turned a blind eye to her behavior all along, put up with the most extraordinary whims, supported her in some things against my better judgment, paid for her to travel abroad when she chose to throw away her expensive education at the Commercial College. I have told myself that not everyone is the same and she has the right to choose her own course, however erratic and bizarre it may seem. In return all I have ever had is ingratitude, as you know. When she was younger she got her own way by pushiness and obstinacy, but over the last few years she has considered your Father's and my opinion unworthy of consulting . . . I thought I had become used to her reproofs, the way she rides roughshod over us, but it has gone too far these last few months, not least after her deception over that Jew. Since then I have asked myself again and again whether she has always gone behind our backs. Whether I can ever trust her. Whether she knows herself when she's telling the truth and when she's lying . . .

I put down the letter and stood motionless for a long time. I must have continued to fiddle with the necklace because I suddenly became aware of it cutting into my neck. I flinched and it snapped. I was trembling so much when I went to fetch my coat that I had to carry it downstairs and only put it on when I stepped into the cold. The letter was in my pocket.

It wasn't until I opened the front door to 56 Fjolugata that I realized I had left the baby alone in the flat.

The day the British occupied Iceland the mistress took to her bed. She had invited me to a piano concert at the Old Cinema the previous evening, as Dr. Bolli was playing bridge at Vilhjalmur Borg's house. It was a beautiful evening with a dark blue tint over the mountains and gentle ripples out in the bay, so she suggested walking home after the concert. I remember that we walked hand in hand. When we drew near the lake we saw theatergoers flocking out of the old theater into the mild evening air. There was a new comedy showing and everyone looked happy. The mistress said: "Disa, isn't it wonderful that spring is on the way?"

For the last few days the weather had been overcast, sometimes with a dusting of snow during the night, but now swans flew above their reflection in the lake and a couple we met at the concert said they had just come from their spring chores at the allotments down on the marsh.

"Isn't it wonderful that spring is on the way?"

But now she was laid up and my employer was rushing around town and couldn't take care of her. At first she refused to eat, but in the evening Maria brought me a mes-

sage from her saying she wanted some soup. I have sometimes wondered since why she didn't let me see her when she
was in her worst state, using Maria as a go-between instead. I
see now that it was pride and affection. I'm also sure that it
was better for both of us.

She stayed in bed for almost a week and when she finally
got up, her husband relayed to us her wish that the occupation should not be mentioned in the household. If she was
nearby, we were careful, for instance, not to switch on the
wireless during the news and made sure that the newspapers
weren't left lying around. Maria read to her from the morning paper, mainly the obituaries and articles of general interest, and the mistress would turn her back to her so that she
couldn't see the front page.

Maria and I told each other that this isolation must end
soon. For the first weeks of the occupation, the mistress didn't
leave the house, but at the beginning of June her doctor rang
and asked her to come to his surgery. I'm pretty sure it was a
deliberate ploy on his part to make her come to him, rather
than visiting her at home in Fjolugata as he usually did.

We were tense while she was out, dreading the worst. It
therefore surprised us how calm she was when she returned
after an hour or so. "Perhaps she's accepted the inevitable,"
suggested Maria, but I guessed that the doctor had given her
some stronger drugs than usual.

The mistress said she'd kept her eyes closed in the car on
the way down to the town center where the doctor had his
surgery. At his prompting, however, she had opened them
on the way home. She described the troops in the lorry outside Hotel Borg as if she were telling us news, the sandbags
which had been piled up against the cellar windows at the
Post Office and the air-raid shelters on the hill. Her voice was
low and her eyelids were heavy. Shortly afterward she fell
asleep in a chair in the drawing room.

We were relieved and hoped that the worst was now over. So it came as a shock how badly she reacted to the first air-raid drill a week later.

Dr. Bolli had warned her but she didn't mention to Maria or me that she was dreading the practice. It began after midday with the sirens giving the warning signal, a constantly varying tone at first, followed by frequent sharp blasts. Several minutes later every telephone in the town rang for thirty seconds altogether. It was at that point that she had a fit.

"Bolli!" she screamed. "Bolli . . ." raising her voice as usual on the final syllable.

He was at her side and yet she continued to call for him.

She never got used to the drills, though she never again reacted quite as badly as that first time. As for me, I tried to prepare myself for them as well as I could. When I look back I can't help concluding that her reaction was my salvation to a certain extent. Although the war had now chased me to Iceland and memories ambushed me at every step, worrying about her provided me with a certain comfort. Yes, I think she was my salvation.

In the middle of June I came across her in the drawing room. She was wearing a yellow dressing gown decorated with pictures of white birds, and had her back turned to the door. On the table at her side lay a copy of the morning paper.

"Atli," I heard her say over and over again. "Atli, my darling boy."

Shaken, I hurried into the kitchen to distract my thoughts.

Late in the summer of 1940 two officials became frequent visitors to Fjolugata. In fact, quite a few so-called men of influence were in the habit of visiting Dr. Bolli, generally for advice or support. This time, however, there was something unusual going on. My employer seemed not merely preoccupied but sometimes positively anxious. His smile was unusually distant and there was no glint in his eye when he tried to maintain his custom of making a little joke with me whenever he had the opportunity. Though he moved around quietly and tried to avoid waking anyone, I would hear him get out of bed night after night. I always slept lightly, remaining on my guard. Why, I don't know. One night when I went down to the kitchen to fetch a glass of milk, I saw him standing in his office with the lights off, staring at the gray light which filtered in through the window. Like a statue, with his hands behind his back, until dawn. Then at last he sat down and was still asleep in his office chair when Maria arrived at eight. His mind was far away and he would lose the thread in mid-sentence, saying: "Asdis, two men will be coming to talk to me later today . . . if you wouldn't mind . . . three o'clock . . . if you . . . ," losing the thread and staring into space until I asked: "Three o'clock? Three o'clock, Dr. Bolli?" Then he'd come to himself and say, "Yes, some cakes, maybe. There'll be two of them. Maybe some cakes with the coffee, if you wouldn't mind."

They came to see him, and it was obvious that this time they were not seeking his support but helping him. I heard them say: "We'll do what we can. The ship is to depart from Finland. Petsamo is the name of the town. In the far north of Lapland. But first he'll have to get to Copenhagen . . . We'll have to ask the German embassy in Denmark to mediate, preferably Ambassador Renthe-Fink himself . . . Georgia will be making the journey too but her son Bjorn's staying on in Germany . . ."

When the Germans invaded Denmark in April, shipping between Iceland and Denmark was suspended, trapping many Icelanders in Copenhagen who were waiting to come home. Georgia was the wife of the Sveinn Bjornsson, the Icelandic ambassador to Denmark. He was to become Iceland's first president in 1944 when the country declared its independence from Denmark. I had heard that their son Bjorn and Atli were very friendly.

"We'll have to get a message to Atli. We'll contact Vilhjalmur Finsen in Stockholm. He passes on messages to Jon Krabbe in Copenhagen. Jon gets on well with Renthe-Fink."

And he saw them off with the long, hard handshake of a man who knew he had no choice. Feeling he was drowning, he hung on tight to the one slender rope that someone threw him out of a sense of duty.

For some reason, the mistress was livelier than usual these days. She generally rose before noon, dressed and came downstairs, sometimes going out into the garden to look at the birds and plants, saying to me when she appeared in the kitchen doorway: "Disa, imagine, it's getting warmer at last!"

She would sit at the corner table and I'd watch her in the mirror as I stood over the pans on the stove, wondering whether I could do anything to cheer her up. Sometimes she would tell me of her childhood in the west of the country, of trips abroad, a room at the Angleterre which she said she was particularly fond of. She seldom asked me anything about myself, perhaps from indifference but more likely out of consideration. The cup she drank coffee from was blue with a picture of a tree in the middle of a field, the only one left from a set her mother had owned. She drank her coffee slowly, popping a sugar lump in her mouth from time to time, always with the same words: "perhaps I'll just sneak one more . . ."

The visits to my employer lasted for more than a fortnight but it was not until the last few days that Maria thought she guessed their purpose. She had to put two and two together because they generally fell silent when she brought them refreshments, waiting for her to leave before resuming their conversation.

"It's the son," she said. "He's in some fix in Germany. Dr. Bolli's trying to get him home via Denmark."

I cut off the conversation as quickly as I could but that night I slept unusually badly. "My darling Jakob," I whispered to myself repeatedly, weeping into the pillow so that no one would hear. "Oh, Jakob, Jakob." Unable to reach out a helping hand, utterly useless.

"It's the son," said Maria. "I'm sure it's him." "Cakes and coffee," said my employer. "The morning sunshine was so beautiful when it shone through the windows of the Angleterre in Copenhagen." "Come on in," called Jakob. "I won't pinch your toes, I promise . . ."

A restless night, full of voices in fragmented dreams. And the dawn all too far away.

Maria had warned me. "It doesn't happen often," she said, "but at least once a year. Usually in the spring or autumn. In the Easter blizzards, for example, or when it's growing colder in September and the grass is fading and the trees are all bare and dismal."

"Celebrate Christmas?" I exclaimed when she came to me in the kitchen after seeing the mistress upstairs. "Now? This evening?"

Dr. Bolli had gone out east the previous day and wasn't expected home until after the weekend. When he said good-bye I noticed that he had lost weight. The same could not be said of his visitors from the government.

"You should see how they stuff themselves with your cakes," said Maria. "It's impossible to tell which of them eats more."

Before my employer left, a premonition stole into my mind, as when the whispering of ghosts troubles one between sleeping and waking. A vague suspicion that some change was imminent. Unconfirmed, of course, and no doubt groundless, as I told myself.

202

The mistress's orders, on the other hand, were clear. She wanted the Christmas lights put up, candles placed in candlesticks, the gramophone moved down to the drawing room and Bach's Christmas Oratorio put on at one o'clock and played until six. The silver was to be polished, the china plates brought out and the table laid for three. She asked Maria not to forget to go out into the garden and cut some pine needles, dry them and carry them burning around the house to make a nice smell. I got in touch with my Danish friend in Hafnarfjordur and asked him to supply me with ptarmigan and smoked lamb.

"It's Christmas!" she cried. "Now we'll have some fun!"

She had asked the hairdresser to come and see her at three o'clock and Maria was worried that the woman would see the Christmas decorations and gossip. So we postponed decorating the front room and entrance until she had left.

"And cinnamon, Disa. Something with cinnamon. I do so love the smell."

"Baked apples?"

"Yes, what a very good idea."

"Ptarmigan and smoked lamb!" said the Dane. "Are you celebrating Christmas or something?"

I didn't answer but could tell that he knew what was going on.

"Do give my regards to the mistress."

When Bach was on the gramophone and the smoked lamb in the pan, when Maria had walked around the house with the crackling pine needles and lit the Christmas lights in the dining room, it suddenly felt as if we had both been lifted by the festive atmosphere out of the gloomy spring day into a warm, merry glow. We became inadvertent participants in the game, suggesting that we should put the angel candles on the sideboard in the dining room and the fir branches in a vase in the drawing room, then dressing in our best clothes later in the day, drinking toasts in port with the mistress at six o'clock and wishing each other a merry Christmas.

We dined at seven. The mistress wore a blue silk dress with white pearls at her throat. They cast a glow on her face and in the candlelight I saw how beautiful she must have been when she was younger. We sang "Silent Night" and then tucked into lobster soup followed by the smoked lamb and ptarmigan.

After dinner we sat in the drawing room with coffee, port and biscuits. The mistress handed each of us a present and we were embarrassed at not having bought anything for her. She gave me a brooch and Maria a scarf. We played whist till late, in the highest of spirits. As the evening wore on the wind began to blow and every now and then a cloudburst poured down. Judging from the rattle on the windows, the downpour was mingled with hail. But we didn't let it affect us because we were merry and the port warmed us to the core.

"No trump," said Maria.

"I say. And you, Disa?"

"I've got a useless hand."

The shadows which assailed her were far away at this moment and a calm glow lit her face. Her eyes were peaceful. She took a pebble from the table and stroked it between her fingers, softly as if it were fragile or held some sort of answer.

"He gave it to me as a Christmas present when he was five," she said finally. " 'It's a wishing stone, Mother,' he said. 'You can wish for anything you like.' "

For a while she continued to caress the stone with the thumb of her right hand, then put it carefully aside.

"He's always been sensitive. Always. He's not suited to these political squabbles. This war . . . Thank God, he's coming home."

204

We didn't stop playing until the candles began to burn down one after another. Then we thanked each other for the evening with kisses and retired to bed.

As I shut my eyes, yet another cold squall battered against the window.

A letter from Anthony, dated July 24, 1940, written on faded blue paper. Somehow it has found its way on this journey with me and so has now come to Iceland for the second time. I read it with half my mind, the rest occupied with the view from my window here at Hotel Borg; over the square which looks awfully desolate in early morning, and the profile of the independence hero's statue, which hasn't changed at all since the last time I saw it.

I've had no news of Jakob despite various attempts to investigate, he wrote. *I've been told it's a difficult undertaking—hopeless, some say, but I ignore them—to try and get news of people who have been sent to prison camps. But of course, I won't give up and will write again in a fortnight, as usual.*

I'm not going to depress you with any new accounts of the situation in London; nothing's changed since I last wrote. There's next to nothing to tell of my own news, the sun rises and sets and sometimes I get a visitor to cheer me up.

Yesterday I received a letter from my cousin who is stationed just outside Calcutta. He was on leave and wrote to me from the bar of the Great Eastern.

206

Although he hasn't yet seen any action, his letter served to remind me of how useless I am. Stuck in this ludicrous desk job. I know I'll never be sent into battle.

I try to play tennis at least twice a week and have taken part in the odd cricket match this spring. I sometimes play bridge with the Old Bridge Farm crowd, the Wakefields and their relatives, to pass the time while the world burns . . .

David took a trip down here last week and stayed with me over the weekend. He's showing the effects, blaming himself for not having gone to Germany instead of Jakob, usually in silence but out loud when he's been drinking, and that's more often these days than is good for him. How different they are, those brothers, Jakob so strong and reliable . . . But no more about that.

By the way, an acquaintance of mine at the Foreign Ministry told me an extraordinary story about David's girlfriend Anna. (Ex-girlfriend, I should add.) Extraordinary, I say, but somehow I don't think you'll be surprised. As you know, she was never short of a shilling, coming from such a well-to-do family. The story doesn't mention where her parents are now but Anna is a passenger on a Dutch ship sailing between Amsterdam and New York. Naturally you will ask if she is on her way to America. And the answer is: sometimes and sometimes not. Apparently, there are quite a number of Jewish girls playing this game, most of them married with husbands in prison camps. The crews call them "water babies" and treat them like ladies, and there's nothing coincidental about which officer gets which girl on each voyage. They have actually got up a rota system which is strictly adhered to. The captain chooses first, then the first engineer, and so on down the line. However, they are not allowed to have the same girl for more than two voyages in a row. This is to prevent the relationship from becoming too close. The girls are thought to dance well and ornament the tables—and more than that, I expect. They sail in this way back and forth across the Atlantic and when the ship puts into port they don't go ashore, just read newspapers and magazines and order their clothes over the phone. If they hear of some of their girlfriends aboard another ship in the same harbor, they get in touch. Always by phone, as they don't dare to leave the ship.

I didn't mention Anna to David. Things are bad enough . . .

I put down the letter. The last I heard of David was that he was living on the east coast of America, possibly in New York. I've had no news of Anna and made no attempt to obtain any.

Two gulls take to the air over the independence hero, who pays them no attention but continues to contemplate the façade of the parliament building. I slept well until four o'clock this morning but have been lying awake ever since. Perhaps I'll take a painkiller at six. It's ten to, now.

A workman crosses the square carrying his lunch pail. I watch him appear, grow larger, shrink and finally disappear in the direction of the harbor. I reach out for the telephone directory. Atli Bollason, managing director, 22 Havallagata. Respectable, no doubt, the father of two or three children, probably running to fat, a sober pillar of the community, his wife standing meekly at his side, remaining silent while he talks. Gazing at him with admiring eyes. 22 Havallagata.

It's five to six. I can't wait any longer. I gulp down two painkillers and close my eyes in the faint hope of sleep.

My relationship with my sister Jorunn began to break down the day I left her daughter alone in her flat. I apologized many times and tried to make her understand what effect Mother's letter had had on me but it just made things worse. Sometimes I persuade myself that everything would have been different if Mother's letter hadn't been left lying in the middle of the sitting room table—wrapped in a yellow ribbon for all to see—but I have to admit that this is a lame excuse. Perhaps ignorance and self-deception are the best insurance for a happy life, and so it would be best to leave this world in perfect ignorance of what was true and what false. After all, the truth has often proved a poor provision on my journey.

Jorunn never blamed me openly but I knew very well how she felt inside. And I wasn't in any doubt about her husband Gunnar's attitude. I don't blame him. In spite of this, he was polite to me on the occasions when I met them after that, which was not often. As a result, Jorunn's illness largely passed me by. After I returned to England we didn't communicate until 1952 when we began to write to each other again. This was after Anthony had urged me to take the initiative and send the first letter. I remember writing to her about the arrival of spring in Somerset, the plants and birds, trout streams and Tina, then just a puppy. For the first months I ignored some of the signs in her letters, omens and strange premonitions, but as time went on I couldn't look the other way any longer. Although sometimes it wasn't obvious that anything was wrong with her, increasingly often I was able to read between the lines and sense her indisposition and anguish, usually over something trivial, and her fear of everything and nothing. I tried, in other words, to ignore it at first, telling myself, for instance, that I had bad days myself but in the end I couldn't avoid facing up to the fact that my sister Jorunn was not in a good way. By then we had been corresponding for nearly a year and when I reread her first letters and compared them with the ones I'd received recently, there was no question that the shadows on her soul had grown longer and darker. After taking advice from Anthony and a friend of ours who was a doctor, I decided to seize the bull by the horns and ask her what was the matter in a letter which I sent early in September. I did my best to word it carefully so as not to hurt or offend her in any way. I even took the letter to the post office myself as if this would somehow have an effect on how it was received.

I awaited the reply with trepidation. The postman usually came in the late morning and I waited in the hall on those days when I expected a letter. Our staff had begun to notice this behavior, since it was as if I had become a fixture in the hall. They started to put their heads together and try to guess what was going on. But as the weeks passed without sign of an envelope bearing her elegant handwriting, I became filled with weary despair and stopped waiting for the kitchen clock to strike eleven as a sign that the time had come for the arrival of the post. I regretted having sent the letter, trying to remember what I had said and what I had omitted, regretting not having memorized it better. Perhaps I should have been more tactful, I told myself, perhaps I shouldn't have "seized the bull by the horn," as I had persuaded myself was most honest. Had I behaved badly? Opened a wound which had perhaps begun to heal, been guilty of prying yet again?

So I wallowed in doubt and tortured myself with endless speculation until at last her letter came late in October. It was the day after the first night frost and I remember that the grass was still rimed outside the kitchen window when I sat down by it and summoned the courage to open the envelope.

The explanation for Jorunn's silence was simple—fortunately, I want to say, though I know it may sound strange. She had been in the hospital for a month.

I've had this problem for many years, she wrote to me, *but during the last few months it got worse . . . When things began to get in a mess this autumn, Gunnar took charge and had me admitted. I'm feeling much better now. The walls of the labyrinth have receded; they don't menace me any longer, don't close in on me as they did before. I've stopped being afraid they're going to touch me, crush me . . . I've started going out again and don't avoid the neighbors any more, not even the woman in the basement who I thought was stalking me, or the man who always stood by the post boxes as if he were waiting for a letter which never came. He's disappeared now. Perhaps he never existed except in my head . . .*

Disa, sometimes I used to sit in the same chair all day long, staring into space. I can't describe how bad I felt. I thought I was worthless, worthless, couldn't see any hope in this life. It was as if I didn't care about anything or anyone—not even Helga, but you must never tell her that. Whatever happens, you must never do that, because you know how much I love her, you know she's everything to me. But that's what this illness is like, this nightmare . . .

She didn't refer to her illness except in the past tense. I was terribly relieved. Anthony mentioned at the supper table that I seemed more cheerful than I had for weeks.

"She's been given drugs for depression," I told him. "It's all over now."

But no sooner had I crawled into bed toward midnight than I began to doubt the efficacy of the cure. It became apparent that she would never be rid of the illness, never completely and never for long. When she was feeling better she was in high spirits and welcomed each day with interest and sincerity, took to religion—"now I live in God"—went to meetings, even came to visit Anthony and me, staying with us for a fortnight. It was wonderful to see her so contented, though of course she was on drugs and therefore a little more manic than usual. What good times those were!

And so the years passed in fluctuation between light and shadow, hope and despair. So they passed, until the light went out and the darkness, thick as pitch, closed in on her from all sides.

The day Jorunn committed suicide the sun was shining. My bedroom was stuffy after the heat of the night and I had just opened the window which faces the avenue of trees when Gunnar rang. While we were talking I watched Anthony walk over from the tennis court, dressed in white, wiping the sweat from his forehead as he approached the back door. Although it was a calm day, the curtain fluttered every now and then in some faint puff of breeze which carried to me—as if from duty and custom—the smell of omelette and fried bacon from the kitchen. I suddenly remembered that I had been meaning to say something to Anthony before he came in to breakfast, but couldn't for the life of me recall what it was. I was distracted by this so that I didn't quite understand some of what Gunnar told me, which must have been why I was startled when he said: "Do you think you'll be able to?"

"What?"

"Do you think you'll be able to come to the funeral?"

I can't remember exactly how I answered, doubt in fact whether I made any sense, as I had begun to tremble violently where I stood by the window. I dropped the receiver on the floor and took a long time to stoop down for it, finally grasping it with both hands and saying a hurried good-bye to Gunnar, promising I would ring him later.

I lay curled up on the floor and shut my eyes. Somewhere in the distance I sensed the lapping of waves and smell of seaweed from the shore at home in Kopasker.

"Disa, we'll always be friends, won't we?"

"Yes, always."

"Even when we're grown up?"

"We'll always be friends."

When I was finally able to stand up, it came to me that I had meant to remind Anthony about the scones I had baked the previous evening. They had turned out well, light and soft, perfect for spreading with blackberry jam to accompany his morning tea.

I went down to the kitchen and fetched the scones from the cupboard. Anthony had already eaten, but had two scones out of politeness. I blamed myself for not having remembered them when I saw him coming in from the tennis court.

"Are you alright?" he asked.

"Please try at least one scone, will you?"

It wasn't until that evening that I found strength to tell him of Jorunn's death.

Old Marshall doesn't talk much while he sits with me in the kitchen, looking out of the window. He nurses his cup between his hands, sipping the tea slowly and taking a long time to finish it. He has always been taciturn and people who don't know him sometimes think he's not quite all there. The other day I saw that he had something on his mind. His eyes looked evasive and he drank his tea faster than usual. Eventually he said: "You'll have to look after him when I'm gone."

I knew he meant Anthony.

"You're not going anywhere, old man. You're as strong as an ox. We'll both keep an eye on him together as we always have."

"There's been a strange horse down in the meadow these last few nights," he said after a short silence. "A gray one. I don't know where it comes from and if I watch it for too long it disappears."

He stood up, opened the door and looked out.

"It often stops down by the stream and changes color in the moonlight. Turns blue. If it's come for me, you'll have to look after Anthony."

He turned and looked at me.

I wonder if he suspects anything? I asked myself. Can he tell anything from looking at me?

I glanced away. The clock in the hall struck three deep tones. My face appeared pale in the mirror on the wall.

The morning the son of the house returned home aboard the *Esja,* my mistress gave me the little mirror in the kitchen. She was up unusually early that day and came down to the kitchen just after nine o'clock to have her coffee and tell me that I could have "that little mirror." I don't know what made her do this as I had never given any hints, though I was fond enough of it. I could lose myself in its reflection, vanish back in time with no commitments, forget my troubles and pretend that all was sunshine and light. Sometimes it reminded me of the sky above Kopasker when I was a girl looking for signs and portents. I had never mentioned to the mistress that I coveted the mirror and so it took me by surprise when she referred to it for the first time that morning. Without preamble, I might add, then never mentioned it again. Perhaps she had seen me dusting it and doubtless noticed the shelf I had put up under it for my bits and pieces, lipstick, comb and a feather, but had never seen me looking in it as far as I knew. I only did that when I was alone.

I accepted the mirror gratefully and although I knew I

would never want to move it from its place, it gave me a strange delight to be able to tell myself that it was mine.

At eleven o'clock Dr. Bolli rang from the bank to announce that the *Esja* had anchored in the outer harbor. He said the British authorities still had to check the passengers' passports but when this was done the ship would dock. The mistress got ready to welcome her son.

But the day wore on without the passengers being allowed ashore. Dr. Bolli came home, obviously anxious. Each passenger had been made to give the names of six people in Reykjavik who could give the military authorities information about them. The mistress took to her bed. My employer paced up and down. I overheard him asking someone on the phone whether the government was going to intervene.

The day passed, then the evening, and during the night, instead of going to bed, Dr. Bolli sat in his office in the darkness. I looked in on him once. He was motionless in his chair. I didn't know whether he was asleep, so decided not to speak to him.

The following morning the interrogations took place. The mistress didn't appear but her husband went out before seven. When he rang around midday to let us know that the passengers had finally received permission to go ashore, his voice was so weak that I was shocked. Maria dashed straight upstairs to the mistress and helped her get dressed.

At two o'clock the couple went down to the harbor to meet their son. Maria dusted and finished polishing the silver. I prepared a supper of lobster and goose according to the mistress's instructions. There was lively music on the radio and my mirror and I were in a good mood from listening to it and exchanged arch glances more than once as I stood by the stove.

It was nearly five o'clock when the front door opened. Maria and I went into the hall to greet them, Maria first, with me a little way behind. Father and son said little, it was the mistress who talked. We introduced ourselves. He nodded when he shook our hands, then immediately looked away.

"Well," said the mistress, taking off her hat, which was yellow with a red feather. "Home at last. Atli, dear, won't you . . ."

"I'm going to lie down, Mother."

"That's a good idea. That's a very good idea. It'll do you good to rest before supper. We're having a celebratory meal. After the journey . . . It'll do you good to lie down."

Atli Bollason was of medium height with a round, pale face and tousled hair. He wore a black cloak with an astrakhan collar, a wide-brimmed felt hat on his head and a white scarf around his neck. He dropped the cloak on to a chair in the front room and left the hat and scarf on top of it. The hat fell to the floor but he didn't seem to notice, at least he didn't stop to pick it up but opened the basement door and headed downstairs. I noticed that he had a limp.

"Maria, dear, would you make up a bed for Atli, please."

"There's no need," he said without looking round.

Maria hung up his cloak in the closet and I went into the kitchen. There was a door to the basement from the kitchen pantry and from time to time I heard his footsteps, alternately heavy and light. It surprised me that he hadn't gone to lie down and I began involuntarily to listen. Heavy, light, heavy, light . . . His footsteps echoed in my head until long after he had gone to sleep.

Supper was kept waiting for him and so were his parents. At seven o'clock the mistress asked her husband to go down and fetch him.

My employer got slowly to his feet.

"He's stirring," he said when he came back. "He'll be along in a minute."

They drank sherry. The mistress put Bach on the gramophone, which was still down in the drawing room following our Christmas celebration a fortnight earlier. The mistress talked. Her husband said nothing. At half-past seven she came out and called down the stairs to her son but got no answer. Shortly afterward, Dr. Bolli made a second trip down to the basement. She popped into the kitchen to see me.

"I don't understand this at all, Disa. Won't the food be ruined?"

I tried to calm her, saying I'd throw the lobster in the pan when they were ready to sit down and assuring her that the goose would be better for resting a little.

"He's tired," she said as if to herself. "He's always been so sensitive . . ."

It was past eight o'clock when they finally sat down at the table. The son smoked nonstop, with an ashtray at his side. His mother tried to maintain a flow of conversation. He held the cigarette between the thumb and index finger of his right hand and picked listlessly at his food with the left, sticking the fork absentmindedly on to the plate so it seemed a matter of chance whether he speared a morsel of food. The mistress had asked me to open a bottle of the best red wine in the house, a Ducru-Beaucaillou from before the Great War, but her son chose to drink brandy instead, even with the goose.

The mistress talked.

". . . you were only five years old, Atli dear. Do you remember? 'You can wish for anything you like, Mother,' you said, 'because it's a wishing stone.' Just five years old . . ."

The son lit another cigarette. Maria emptied the ashtray and wiped it clean.

"You and Kristjan played together so often when you were boys. He's working for his father's firm now. I told Mrs. Thorarinsson you were on your way home. She was going to let Kristjan know. You were always such good friends . . . but now he's started working for his father . . ."

It was a monologue rather than a conversation and my employer was so strangely unlike his usual self. He retired to bed just after ten, forgetting to wish me good night for the first time ever. Mother and son remained sitting in the drawing room.

"Shall we play cards?" I heard her ask.

"Later, Mother, later. I'm tired."

He soon fell asleep in his chair. Maria and I helped each other clear up. The mistress came to see us in the kitchen, thanking us for the evening and saying something else complimentary which I've forgotten. Maria left toward midnight.

I was pensive when I went to bed and lay awake for a long time in the light summer night.

I was still thinking of little Marilyn when I woke up this morning. It was nearly eleven o'clock; I must have fallen sound asleep after taking those painkillers. I woke to the sound of a knock at the door—three knocks, I thought I heard—at first light, then more insistent. I felt groggy but got up anyway and put on my dressing gown. There was no one outside in the corridor when I opened the door.

I was late for breakfast but persuaded them to bring me a slice of bread and cheese with my tea. The girl who answered the phone when I rang down to the lobby sounded extraordinarily like Marilyn, quiet and amiable, and I drew out the conversation for the pleasure of listening to her voice.

I've always enjoyed eating breakfast in bed and decided to treat myself for once; after all, I had nothing better to do. There was a small round table below the window and I've moved it over to the bed as my bedside table is too high and, anyway, it's piled up with the papers and documents I've been looking through since I arrived. As I drank my tea I reached out for a cutting which I had brought with me but been too busy to glance at. It wasn't until I heard the sound of that girl's voice in reception that I remembered I had brought it with me on my journey.

Actually, I thought I had got rid of this magazine article and so was astonished when I found it among Marilyn's old letters in the bottom drawer of my bedroom desk the day before I left. It's from the *Daily Telegraph:* September 1959, I have written at the bottom of the cutting, while at the top is the headline *Two Chefs, Two Styles—A Comparison.* Before I go any further I should mention that I no longer believe little Marilyn was behind this article or tried to influence the author. Not deliberately, anyway.

I admit I suspected her of spite when the article first came to my attention and I remember storming up and down, asking myself and Anthony how she could do this to me after all I had done for her. Anthony tried to calm me, convinced that Marilyn had taken no part in this attack on me. His tolerance and trusting nature got on my nerves, however, and I couldn't help accusing him of being gullible and naïve.

"Do you imagine this is a coincidence?" I asked. "An accident, maybe? Are you telling me that Marilyn won't enjoy reading flattering things about herself and slanderous comments about me?"

I find myself becoming worked up by the memory, so I'll slow down, finish drinking the tea I ordered from room service and then try to the best of my ability to describe the contents of this article, the events leading up to it and its consequences. But first I'm going to take a sip of tea and a sugar lump, breathe in deeply as Dr. Ellis taught me and switch on the radio in the hope of hearing some decent music.

Those who knew Nora Gannon generally agreed that she lacked both the judgment and the know-how to write about food. Many also doubted her integrity as her pieces often radiated envy and vulgarity. As with so many others in her situation, she herself had no doubt once dreamed of being able to cook and attempted a career in that field, but judging by her writing she had not been meant for it. It's one thing to want something, another to be capable of it, and not everyone can cope with the disappointment. They become bitter, malicious and petty, with not a good word to say about anything. They try to promote themselves in this way but of course sink only deeper with every attack and end up having to heap even more abuse in order to climb out of the holes they've dug for themselves.

Soft-hearted people tended to tolerate Mrs. Gannon and excused her by saying she was an able writer. I myself find her style pretentious twaddle.

I made no secret of my opinion of Nora Gannon and there was no question that it had come back to her. For the first few years she snubbed me, never mentioning Ditton Hall in her annual articles about summer hotels and restaurants, pretending I didn't exist and naturally losing face herself by her ludicrous behavior. I shrugged it off and in fact had long ceased to think about Mrs. Gannon when she could no longer resist the temptation and wrote the article about me and Marilyn. This was two years after Marilyn had made the move north to Windermere and Mrs. Gannon was "amazed" at how "she had achieved so much in such a short time."

The occasion of the article—if it can be called an occasion —was a party Marilyn held to promote her restaurant to the press. (Whereas it has never actually crossed my mind to do anything of the kind; I've never seen any reason to bribe these people to flatter me.) The party was the intended success, newspapers and magazines competed in their praise of little Marilyn and some even published photographs of her and William, her husband, who looked rather foolish in all the pictures, poor thing. I was pleased for her, even though I knew how she had obtained these accolades and was worried whether she could live up to them. But it never occurred to me that Nora Gannon would stoop so low as to use this opportunity to compare Marilyn's cooking with mine. It shouldn't surprise anyone that in making this comparison Mrs. Gannon broke all her own records of vulgarity and spite. And that took some doing.

Anthony was convinced that little Marilyn had nothing to do with this attack but I couldn't draw the same conclusion until I had thought long and hard. I decided at last that she had probably spoken incautiously to Mrs. Gannon but not deliberately tried to undermine me. She tried repeatedly to get me on the phone after the article appeared but I wasn't at home to her. I forbade Anthony to talk to her but don't know whether he obeyed. After a year or so I decided to make peace with her. I suspect some people would have taken longer.

I put down my pen and reach out for my teacup. The morning paper lies beside the pot: June 15, it says. Graduation tomorrow. What will he look like? I ask myself. Who will he look like? And what shall I say to him? After all these years. What can I say?

The tea is cold but I finish the cup anyway. The skies are gray. I reach for my photo of him.

Sometimes the son of the house would make a brief appearance but otherwise he kept to his two rooms in the basement or wrapped himself in the black cloak, which he must have bought on his travels, and disappeared into town. He reversed the clock, sleeping during the day and waking at night, generally emerging by three in the afternoon to have coffee and read the papers. If he bumped into Maria or me he would nod politely but say little, taking his coffee, papers and cigarettes into the study where he would sit chain-smoking and filling the ashtrays over and over again. He rarely ate supper with his parents, though he did tend to stay at home on the evenings when his father had visitors. He didn't take much part in the conversation during the evening, but would sit in a corner listening to talk, according to Maria, of politics and finance, economic growth and profit, wholesale and retail, Franklin & Svensen—Import/Export, salmon fishing and the overbearing behavior of the damned British. Sometimes he would smile but as the evening drew on and the first cognac bottle had been emptied, he began to let slip the odd comment on what was being discussed. The guests seemed to pay attention to him, not least the swan-loving editor and importer Hallur Steinsson, and his wife's sister's husband, Heimir Frantz, a ship broker. They were extraordinarily alike to look at, Hallur and Heimir, both round-cheeked, stocky rather than fat, of medium height, thinning on top, Heimir beginning to go gray, Hallur still ruddy.

"Quite right," said Hallur whenever he thought something sensibly expressed. "There should be an article written about that."

According to Maria, they sometimes stopped talking when she came in, unsurprisingly, as she brought them refreshments which deserved their attention: coffee and cakes, port and brandy. They would sometimes play cards and Atli would let himself be persuaded to join, even though he described himself as a poor player. For some reason, both Maria and I thought we sensed a degree of perplexity in our employer's demeanor when his son was present. It often seemed as if he needed to talk to him about something, something which had been on his mind, but which he hadn't had a chance to put into words. Sometimes he would clear his throat, sometimes he'd say "well" in a way that implied a follow-up, occasionally he would begin a sentence only to have it fall apart and dry up.

Once I heard him hint that he was worried about the boy. It was Monday and Dr. Bolli came home from the office at midday, asking Maria where his son was as soon as he came through the door. Maria said he was asleep. Without even taking off his coat his father went straight down to the basement. I eavesdropped from the pantry off the kitchen.

"Why didn't you go to the interview?" I heard Dr. Bolli ask. "He waited for you. He postponed a meeting because he was expecting you. And then you didn't turn up . . ."

"Oh, Father. I'm tired."

"In the middle of the day. It's past two o'clock."

"I'm a bit under the weather."

Something must have happened to him, I always thought. I sometimes wanted to ask him what it was that weighed on him, wanted to help because I thought I understood him, even saw Jakob in him, tired and weary. Lethargy, drink and cigarettes —as if he felt best when he was asleep or had dulled his senses. Sometimes he fell asleep in a chair in the corner before the guests had left. Sometimes he had to be helped down to the basement. His father usually came to his aid but once it fell to me.

"Thank you, Asdis," he slurred. "I just don't think I can manage it by myself. Gravity, I mean."

"Maybe you ought to drink less," I ventured.

He smiled.

"Sometimes it's best to know as little as possible."

Once a quarrel broke out between father and son. It was late. They had gone to a party in the afternoon and came home just before eleven. The swan-lover was with them. They asked for coffee and brandy. Hallur Steinsson had a whiskey. They shut themselves in the study. The son of the house and Hallur were both very drunk, though Dr. Bolli didn't appear to be. Atli was talking. He was speaking not loudly but with emphasis. I heard the sound from the kitchen but couldn't catch the words except now and then. Soon Dr. Bolli interrupted. I had never known him to lose his temper but this time he was obviously angry. This discord bothered me but all the same I moved closer to the study.

"I won't listen to such talk," I heard my employer say.

"The boy's right, Bolli," said the swan-lover. "He was asked to pass on this message."

"I won't listen to such talk, Atli," repeated his father. "And it would be better if other people didn't hear it either, after all that's happened."

Silence.

"I'll do what I like."

"Not another word! Not a word!"

I moved away from the door.

"Why don't we just play a game of cards?" suggested Hall-ur. "It's still early."

Dr. Bolli opened the door.

"I think it's bedtime for some people. Atli . . ."

He put his hand under his son's arm and supported him to the basement stairs.

"Leave me alone. I can walk by myself."

"That is a change."

He released him but didn't turn away until the door to the basement had closed.

"It's probably not worth playing cards," said the editor.

My employer fetched his coat and saw him to the door.

"He promised to deliver the message," said Hallur. "He should publish what he's been writing, too."

At that point Dr. Bolli seized the editor by the scruff of his neck and shook him.

"You will never say that again, either to him or anyone else. If I hear it again, I'll hold you responsible."

Hallur Steinsson was distressed as he stumbled out. My employer remained standing in the same spot for a long time after he had gone, before slowly mounting the stairs to his bedroom.

I was about to go to bed when I noticed a light on the basement stairs. When I opened the door to turn it off, there sat the son of the house on the top step, sound asleep. I tried to wake him but it wasn't until after a number of attempts that he opened his eyes.

He gave an unfathomable smile.

"Germany," he said. "We understand what's going on. You and I."

I helped him down the stairs. He lay down fully dressed. When I turned around in the doorway he was asleep.

Anthony said he had bought it in a moment of high spirits when he lived in Paris during the winter of 1930. Though it wasn't cheap, it naturally cost only a fraction of what we got for it when we finally decided to part with it. He said he'd seen it through a window during an afternoon walk on the west bank of the Seine when the rays of the autumn sun had begun to fade and the breeze hinted that the night frost was on its way. He couldn't help noticing it as the sun shone directly on to it where it hung on the wall nearest the window. It wasn't a large picture, but the master's touch was unmistakable. His name was written in tiny letters in the bottom left-hand corner: Picasso, in light blue. The youth—a boy, I think, rather than a girl—was stretching his arms heavenward, fair complexioned, with shoulder-length, red-gold hair. It was a beautiful picture but one we couldn't afford to own. When I first hazarded the suggestion to Anthony that the most sensible thing was probably to sell it, he cut short the conversation immediately. A few years later he pointed out to me that we would have lost a large sum if he had followed my advice, as the picture had steadily increased in value. He was right and I regretted the fact, knowing how much easier our lives would have been had we sold it. Every time I passed the picture in the library it reminded me of my defeat. I began to look askance at it. Just you wait, I told it. Just you wait.

When we decided to make a start on the changes to the east wing and games room in the main house, it just so happened that Anthony received an offer for the picture which he couldn't refuse. I had, naturally, prepared the ground, as shortly before one of our guests had got talking to me in order to angle after it. He was a wealthy American called Lloyd, who had made his fortune in the canned goods business, from what I could gather. I welcomed his interest as we were in dire need of cash. He mentioned a large sum and raised it three times after we had chatted for a while. When I finally told him that sadly I didn't have the authority to arrange the sale and that he himself would have to raise the matter with Anthony, he seemed annoyed but recovered quickly, especially as I promised to give his offer my vote if Anthony consulted me. I also thought I'd better whisper to him that it wouldn't be wise to mention our chat to Anthony.

After Mr. Lloyd had left with the Picasso, I once came upon Anthony standing in front of the blank wall and staring at the patch where the picture of the youth had hung. I'm ashamed to say it but at that moment I felt almost jealous. When he became aware of me, he said, as if in explanation: "I always felt as if the boy were reaching out to the Almighty."

I felt jealous again but was able to hold back.

"While we were clutching at thin air," I said to myself and left him standing by the blank wall.

The voice still whispers in my mind: You have only yourself to blame.

Relentless whispers in my half-waking state, when the moon hovers above me like a lantern in the wind and also when evening comes and the sun withdraws in shame behind a cloud. Relentless whispers, chasing me, hounding me: What did you expect? You have only yourself to blame.

Fleeing from one place to another, resting by a cold wall, far from the merciless glare which spares nothing. The corridors offer shelter, as does the conservatory and the bridge over the brook when my face, reflected in the deep water, floats away.

Then I'm free. At last.

"Asdis, we understand each other. You and I. We know what's going on."

I see the beast between waking and sleeping, feel its breath on my cheek, hot and moist, slow at first, then frantic with lust, feel its tongue lick my throat, sense the terror. The groans were predictable, the shudder of pleasure which shook his body, the silence and emptiness when it was all over.

"I was lucky, Asdis. But I don't want to talk about it. Too difficult. Home at last. So much behind me."

The mistress asleep and my employer out, Maria visiting her sister out east.

"Asdis, would you mind helping me downstairs? My right leg sometimes aches. If you wouldn't mind . . ."

Only a faint smell of alcohol on his breath that evening—he said he'd been to a concert. Yet he wants me to help him. Puts his arm round my shoulders. I hold him round his waist.

"Jakob," I say to him. He's surprised. "Atli," I correct myself, "the last step."

The door opens into the bedroom. I lead him to the bed.

"Won't you sit down here beside me, Asdis? I was lucky. I've come home."

His breath on my neck, gentle and hesitant, disconnected words. I close my eyes.

"Disa, swim to me," says Jakob. "I want to show you something."

"What?"

"Come here. Then you'll find out."

"What?"

Brown eyes? Blue eyes? I can't decide.

"Come here."

His hands move up from my hips under my blouse, stopping at my breasts.

"Lie down."

"Come here," I hear Jakob call in the distance. He's out in the middle of the pond, ducking under the water every now and again, popping up when least expected. Smiling.

"Come here, Disa."

The reflection shatters on the trembling surface of the water.

He enters me. His breathing is rapid and eager, his hands fumble over my body, hot with desire. His tongue licks my

233

throat and chest. When he takes my nipples in his mouth, his hair flops against me, soaked with sweat.

I swim to him and put my arms around him. He raises his hand out of the water. He's holding a bunch of flowers.

"Did you pick them for me?"

"What did you think I was going to do? Tickle you?"

He grabs me and shakes me, I can't escape, don't try to escape, don't scream, don't ask him to stop, don't moan a single word.

He loosens his grasp and subsides. Gets up.

I come to myself. He's standing in front of me, pulling up his trousers, wiping the sweat from his brow with his right sleeve.

"You should visit me more often down here in the basement."

In my dream, the flowers are withered when Jakob hands them to me.

I tried to avoid the son of the house after that. Fortunately, I saw him less often than before because he had procured himself an old car and spent weeks at his parents' summer cottage at Thingvellir. He took advantage of the lack of snow, coming to town from time to time to fetch provisions and have his washing done. Once I remember he rang from Hotel Valholl and asked for his father. My employer was on the phone for a long time, talking first to Atli, then to the caretaker, I suspect. I heard him promise to send money to cover his son's expenses.

"He's always been a nature lover," said his mother, but I thought Dr. Bolli frowned when the conversation turned to these trips to the summer cottage. No doubt the whiskey crate in the boot of the car had something to do with it. He had also recently taken on two high school girls for extra coaching in German but seemed now to have forgotten them. One of them obviously attended these lessons as the result of parental pressure and seemed only too happy when they were cancelled. Her fellow pupil, a pretty brunette sixteen years old, was more persistent, however, and at first rang almost daily to ask for "Atli." Her tone took me by surprise, then I forgot it and didn't think of the girl again until later.

There's no need to go into detail about the sort of state I was in following that evening in the basement. I sometimes ask myself whether I had a soft spot for him, but can't follow the thought through. I give up when I remember New Year's Eve a month later, and feel dirty.

But I do know I was convinced by then that some misfortune haunted him. I imagined that he had been treated harshly in Germany; he had hinted at this but never said so directly. The dullness in his eyes and his apathy, the smile which was not a smile but a painful grimace, the damp, weak handshake—all seemed to me to point the same way.

Brown eyes? Blue eyes? I can't see. Perhaps the eye sockets contain only darkness.

Childishness, I want to say and draw a line through my behavior without further obligation or anguish. So long ago, I want to say, everything's changed. But nothing's changed and two decades are no time. You grow up, people say, as if they have attained some higher wisdom, and will even put on a solemn face if they are sufficiently dishonest with themselves, or else mutter the assertion in low tones, avoiding looking in the mirror.

In the evenings I tried to distract myself by listening to the radio, as I found it difficult to concentrate on a book and didn't seek out company. I hardly saw Jorunn, though I spoke to her on the phone from time to time, but the conversations were short, though polite. Father and I wrote regularly. He said Mother was not in good health but I doubted this. Sometimes I managed to pick up broadcasts by the BBC, especially late in the evening before midnight, and in addition the British started to bring us news of the war in Icelandic at the beginning of December 1940. I had to force myself to sit through those reports.

I can't tell exactly when I gave up hope of seeing Jakob again. Perhaps I had long ago given up, without realizing it. I sensed that Anthony's letters left a lot unsaid, so cautious was he when he told me, for example, of David's fruitless investigation or of his own conversation with officials in London who had nothing encouraging to tell him. "But," he always added, "we must hope for the best."

Hope is the sister of self-deception and I have learned to avoid those sisters as far as I can. Their smile is fawning and their manner false, they give many promises but keep few of them. Nowadays I will make a detour especially to avoid them—for example, pleading with Dr. Ellis to spare me from half-truths. He got rather tangled up but eventually managed to avoid lying. I remember him standing up and going to the window, pausing to look out, twisting an ancient fountain pen between the fingers of his left hand while he ran the right through his thinning hair.

The truth demands accuracy and concentration which sometimes makes it hard to handle.

"Eighteen months," he said eventually.

"Eighteen? Are you sure?"

"Twelve to eighteen."

"I'll take twelve."

This evening I mean to take a taxi over to Fjolugata. I'm not going to get out, just ask the driver to stop by the fence so that I can look at the house, and especially the garden, in peace. I want to recall the light in the garden, which used sometimes to be my only entertainment when I sat in my room in the evenings; a light blue shade in summer under the trees and among the shrubs; peat-brown in the autumn like rain-soaked heaps of leaves or the greatcoats of British soldiers. I'm going to go there this evening because I'm ready to hear echoes from the past and to see a white face at the window. I'm not afraid of anything because I'm ready.

I'm ready for anything.

Early in December I felt as if I'd received a message that Jakob was dead.

Gabriel Turville-Petre of the BBC had finished his address, and the sound of the *Moonlight Sonata* flooded from the radio. Outside it was windless with a heavy drizzle, but in the distance the remnants of a glow could be glimpsed between the clouds. When I looked out into the garden I saw a cat dragging its prey behind it across the lawn. It moved slowly, stopping now and then to get a better purchase on the bird, which struggled at first. But gradually the fight went out of it and by the time the cat had vanished into the next-door garden, the fight was over.

I sat for a long time in the twilight. In the evening it began to pour, turning into a storm during the night. The following day there were puddles on the frozen ground.

After the war David came down to Somerset to tell us that he had received confirmation of his brother Jakob's death. Listening to him was like reading an old newspaper. It had no effect on me.

I don't suppose he understood.

"Bad influenza," wrote Father, but I ignored it as I suspected he was trying to blow up Mother's cold out of all proportion. During the past few months he had made various attempts to make peace between us and I had become suspicious. But when he rang a few days later I knew what he would say as soon as Maria called me.

"Your Mother is dangerously ill," he said. "She's asking for you to come."

It was December 20. We were in the middle of the Christmas preparations. At the mistress's request we had decorated the house in the middle of the month so it was already festive. Jorunn had asked me to dine with her, Gunnar and Helga on Christmas Eve but I declined since I knew that she had invited me only out of a sense of duty. But now she had gone north to be at Mother's side, taking Helga with her.

It was difficult for me to get away so close to Christmas. The mistress had arranged to hold four dinner parties over the holiday season and, in addition, Dr. Bolli had invited the bank staff to a cocktail party on the 30th. I was looking forward to cooking something more substantial at last as the mistress had had little appetite recently and Dr. Bolli always wanted something simple. The call therefore came at the worst possible time. On top of this, I still couldn't help suspecting Father of exaggerating Mother's condition.

The scheduled buses to Akureyri did not run in winter but Dr. Bolli came across a notice in the newspaper saying that Kristjan Kristjansson would be driving his bus north the following day with a few passengers as conditions were good and the roads were clear. I received this news with mixed feelings but I had to go.

The morning was still and gardens and pavements were pale after the night's heavy snowfall. When I climbed into the bus I had a moment of panic as the faces of the other passengers looked odd to me. It may seem unbelievable but I was half afraid of them. In my agitation I dropped my suitcase out of the door and almost fell after it, before getting a better grip, climbing in and sitting by the window near the back.

Lights shone in a few houses on the way out of town but most lay in darkness as it was not yet eight o'clock. I couldn't get rid of the sense of dread which had assailed me as I entered the bus. It grew worse once we were under way and I knew there was no turning back. By the time we trundled over the river on the outskirts of the city, I was on the verge of asking the driver to stop and let me out. Unfortunately, I did nothing.

I closed my eyes and tried to forget my surroundings. It seemed as if dawn would never break, and the moon I saw on the way out of town had vanished behind a cloud. The bus rattled along with the wind howling past the windows, and the fjord looked deep, dark and menacing. Sometimes I sensed mountains and hills in the darkness, the odd farm in a white wasteland, a faint glow in a window, breath on the glass. And eyes staring out.

I don't know where we were when the accident happened. The dawn brought an uncomfortable glare so I had shut my eyes. I think I must have dozed off. When the driver pulled his emergency brake, I was flung against the back of the seat in front of me, while the bus skidded in a circle on the road before finally stopping at the edge.

"A horse!" someone shouted. "We ran into a horse!"

I struggled to my feet. A little boy, who was traveling with his father, lay on the floor beside me. He had a scratch on his forehead but started crying only when his father took him in his arms. The driver asked if anyone was hurt, before hurrying outside with several of the passengers. My shoulder ached from the blow but I followed them anyway as I found it hard to breathe inside the bus. It had begun to snow. There was blood on the road but the horse was nowhere to be seen. We followed its trail to a hillock a short distance from the road but couldn't see the animal anywhere.

"It was white," said the driver.

"White?"

"Yes, I thought it was white. But I'm not completely sure."

We turned back. The wind was rising and the snow whirled up in the arc of the headlights.

"We can't hang around here," said the driver. "I'll report the horse when we get to Akureyri. Thank God, it wasn't any worse."

The boy had stopped whimpering and now lay on his father's lap. People were silent, the snow fell heavily and the bus groaned without relief.

"She'll start," the driver reassured us. "I've often seen it worse."

It was evening by the time we made our slow progress over

the river into Akureyri. The passengers breathed a sigh of relief and praised the driver. He was pleased.

"Let's hope the boat will be able to sail tomorrow morning," he said to me when we parted.

I took a room at Hotel Akureyri. A picture of the harbor hung above the bed.

Outside, the snow kept falling.

Soft flakes obliterated the street and the bench on the pavement opposite. The milkman must have just put the churns by the main entrance farther down the street, as the tracks of his horse and cart were still only half covered. I thought I could see where he had turned the corner and amused myself by following his tracks with my eyes, leaning closer to the glass to follow them right up to the hotel. There was frost on the windowpane and when the tip of my nose touched it a shiver ran through me. At the same moment the light on the bedside table went out and I heard a commotion among the staff downstairs. There was a power outage. I dressed in the gloom; my clothes were cold after the night and I put both hands on the radiator in the corner to warm up. Then I went downstairs.

Candles had been lit in reception and also in the room where breakfast was served. Out on the fjord the wind drove white-frothing waves before it. I was told that the boat to Kopasker could not put out to sea and it was uncertain when it would sail.

"It's anyone's guess when the wind will drop," said the girl who had checked me in yesterday evening. "But Stefan's going to take a look anyway at ten."

I didn't know who Stefan was but suddenly overcome by a sense of claustrophobia I had to get outside. It was around seven o'clock. I was the only person about as I waded through the drifts. The decorations in the shop windows reminded me that it was Christmas Eve. I had forgotten. When I reached the town square the lights suddenly came on in the Christmas tree, then went out a moment later, leaving the tree desolate and sad looking.

There were three of us who had intended to carry on, me and a middle-aged couple on their way to visit their daughter not far from Kopasker. When I came back inside they were sitting with the hotel manager in the dining room, drinking coffee. It became apparent that he was the father of the girl in reception. I could see the resemblance. The old clock ticked away in the corner, striking wearily every quarter hour. They sneaked a glance at it. Half-past eight.

"Stefan's going to take a look at ten o'clock," explained the manager. "He's not afraid of anything, old Stefan. Oh no. Nothing scares him."

The couple asked whether he meant Stefan Gudlaugsson. The manager nodded. They spent the next few minutes discussing his family tree.

"We weren't expecting any guests tonight," said the manager finally. "We'd meant to be finished by midday. But you're welcome to eat with us this evening. To join our family," he added, almost formally.

The couple murmured their thanks, the woman wiping a drip from her nose. I asked the manager if he knew when Kristjan Kristjansson would be driving back to Reykjavik.

"Kristjan? He's planning to stay here over the holiday with his family."

I was determined to take the first bus out of there. Especially if it was heading for Reykjavik. I should never have come on this journey, I told myself, never have let myself be talked into it. Father's anxiety is probably unfounded. And here am I, snowed in at Akureyri where I don't know a soul except Aunt Stina whom I would probably avoid even if she was the last person left on earth. Here I am, unable to leave, far away from my duties and my dear mirror, the stove which I love despite its many failings, and the mistress who was depending on me to do my job during the festivities. Here I am and the silence is strange, and forebodings of failure are unavoidable, the suspicion that soon the peace will be shattered.

My thoughts went round in circles and without warning I began to feel repelled by my fellow travelers, that harmless couple on the way to see their daughter. What if they were talking about me while I was outside? With the manager and his daughter. What if they were pretending they knew something they shouldn't, as if they had heard something they thought I wanted to hide, a whisper in some dark corner? Their eyes seemed shifty and hesitant as if they knew they had done something wrong. I stopped in the doorway and stared at them in silence until they looked in my direction and the manager twisted round in his chair, saying: "Won't you sit down with us and have a cup of coffee? You could do with one after your walk."

And then I realized I was losing control of my thoughts and became afraid.

"In a moment," I said. "I'm just going to get rid of my coat."

By the time I came down, the coffee was cold.

When Jorunn rang to tell me that Mother was dead, it had stopped snowing. It was nearly six o'clock and people were on their way to church. I don't know exactly when it cleared up—I must have been preoccupied—but I don't think it was until after darkness had fallen. I had opened the window in my bedroom and sat down beside it to pass the time. I was feeling weak after the day's anxieties and so sat longer by the window than I had intended, an hour, perhaps more. A little boy came skipping after his parents past the hotel; he was wearing a coat that was far too big for him, probably a hand-me-down. I heard him whining to his parents and amused myself by eavesdropping.

"Please, Mum, please. Just one. Let me open just one present before supper."

I heard the phone ring downstairs before the hotel manager's daughter came and fetched me. It was loud and peremptory. I guessed what the message would be, as Mother had been failing when Jorunn and I spoke at two o'clock. It was still snowing then but the power had come back on.

"Is everything all right?" asked the manager's daughter when I had finished speaking to Jorunn.

"Yes, it's all right."

"Are you sure?"

"Yes, I'm sure."

"And there's nothing I can do for you?"

"I have everything I need."

"You're sure . . ."

"I'm sure."

". . . that you don't want to eat with us? Otherwise you'll be all alone here this evening. On Christmas Eve," she added, as if I had failed to notice.

I don't think her concern was put on; she obviously felt bad about abandoning me. She had been home and changed into her best dress, returning only to close up the office and tell her father to go home, as they were waiting for him.

"Well, you know where we live if you change your mind. Merry Christmas."

She shut the door quietly behind her, then opened it again a moment later to fetch two Christmas presents which she had forgotten behind the reception desk.

"For Mother and Father," she explained. "Merry Christmas."

Silence. The tolling of the church bells didn't disturb me but merged into the silence in the house like a punctuation mark. Through the window came fragments of a hymn sung nearby, "Silent Night," from what I can remember, apparently sung by a young woman. It didn't disturb me any more than the creaking of the staircase leading to the upper floor; I paused on the bottom step.

"Wouldn't you like to listen to the service on the wireless?" the girl had asked before leaving. "You know where to find it, don't you?"

I thanked her.

"Hopefully the wind will drop tonight," she added as she left. "So you'll be able to continue your journey in the morning."

I climbed two steps higher up the staircase and paused. Shifted the weight from my left foot to my right, listening to the creaking of the boards, then shifted back to the left foot. The clock struck six. I remembered that the stairs creaked more lower down and turned round to test them. Meanwhile I unintentionally recalled Jorunn's words.

"It's such a pity you couldn't get here," she said between sobs. "It's so awful that you two didn't have a chance to say good-bye."

The lower steps creaked louder but suddenly I began to shake and felt as if I were losing my footing. I had to sit down and grip the bars of the banisters to keep from falling.

"After everything that's happened," were her exact words. "Everything that's happened."

And suddenly I realized that now it was too late. Nothing could be taken back, nothing changed. Words I had uttered in anger and resentment now returned to me, attacking me out of the silence like ill omens. I put my hands tight over my ears, but nothing helped, they wouldn't leave me alone, thronging at me one after another, ever louder, ever more merciless.

Nothing could be taken back, nothing changed. Memories that seemed engraved in stone, thoughts which shamed me.

My body continued to shake until long after I'd stopped weeping. I heard people walk past singing, but remained sitting motionless on the stairs, gradually relaxing my grip on the banisters.

Why did everything have to turn out like this? We would never make our peace. I would never be able to tell her how much I loved her.

Never.

When I picture in my mind's eye a white rock bathed in sunshine with a dry twig growing out of a cleft, I almost invariably become depressed and miserable. Yet I perk up in heavy drizzle, calm weather or a gentle breeze, and when the dew settles on the grass and the blades droop after a quiet afternoon shower. The conservatory is dear to me after a rainy night, as are the corridors of the house in my wanderings at the end of a rainy day, especially if I have slept well and not been awakened by restless thoughts in the darkness before dawn.

Brilliant light sometimes throws me off balance but, then again, when the long winter nights are at their blackest, I tend to be lethargic and hopeless. Dusk, on the contrary, soothes my mind and warms my soul. Perhaps it's my imagination but I've always thought the buntings in the poplar seem at their merriest in the twilight rain.

The day Mother was buried was cold. It finally began to grow light around midday. The coffin-bearers cast grotesque, elongated shadows on the white earth. At times they seemed to lag behind their owners. The sunlight blinded me and I raised a hand over my eyes to shade them. Jorunn held the other. She stood at my side, between me and Aunt Stina. Father stood at a distance. The day was too bright, the earth too white and I waited impatiently for the ceremony to end.

Father seemed to have shrunk since I last saw him, diminished and dwindled. He spent long hours sitting in his dispensary and spoke little. Jorunn tried more often than once to talk to me about my quarrel with Mother but I cut short the conversation. I didn't do it roughly, even though I was desperate to change the subject, but I'm still afraid I must have hurt her. She seemed to be on pins and needles and I was worried about her health for a while, but then turned my mind to something else. I was relieved that she hadn't opposed burying Mother before the New Year. I couldn't wait to get back to my duties in Reykjavik.

I thought about those days yesterday when Helga, Jorunn's daughter, drank afternoon coffee with me here at the hotel. I had been of two minds about whether I should get in touch with her, but finally decided to go ahead. I don't regret it—quite the reverse—because we had a really enjoyable time; the girl is both happy and good-natured. I was nervous in case she started to ask me about things I preferred not to rake up in company, but fortunately she turned out to be more interested in England and cookery than the past. No doubt her father had told her all sorts of stories about her mother's family but from what she said I gathered he had taken care not to burden her with details which she didn't need to know. I could tell this from her expression as well.

I felt it was all right to ask after her father's circumstances. She spoke well of him and his second wife, a Danish teacher at the high school. I was startled when she mentioned her stepmother's workplace.

It took me by surprise when she said that my brother Kari

had visited Iceland with his family the previous summer. She said she'd gone to Thingvellir with them and made gentle fun of their clothes, especially Kari's green-checked trousers and white shoes. I told her about the Christmas cards and the reports which accompanied them of the family's doings during the past year but realized that I didn't recall having read anything in them about a trip to Iceland.

Before we said good-bye, I invited her to stay with us at Ditton Hall if she happened to be passing. I'm aware the chances are slim that I'll be there to welcome her, but there's no point in saying any more about that. I hope Anthony won't give up when it happens, I said to myself when she had gone, and I was still pursuing the thought. I hope he'll keep things going. It would make me sad if silence returned to our house. I can't bear to think of it after all I had to go through in order to drive it out in the first place.

We parted with kisses in the lobby, saying good-bye to each other. It was then that she asked me out of the blue, but as if she had given it some thought: "Where is grandmother buried?"

I told her that her grandparents' grave was in the churchyard at Kopasker and advised her to make the trip one day.

"It can be incomparably beautiful there," I told her. "The sky," I added, but lost the thread after a few seconds. "The sky is not the same everywhere."

When she had gone I remembered how relieved I had been when I said good-bye to Jorunn and Father the day after the funeral. Jorunn was carrying Helga and waved to the boat. I waved back. I didn't for a moment dream that I would return to Kopasker two weeks later.

Anthony and I talked on the phone this morning. He was a bit depressed at first but gradually cheered up. I heard hammering somewhere in the distance; he said the carpenters were putting up the last doorframes in the east wing and mending the shutters in the dining room. After a reciprocal weather report, I mentioned to him that I had passed Atli Bollason's house the previous evening when I took a trip by taxi around the town. It's a pretty house, near the Catholic church on the hill, with flowerpots by the entrance full of pansies turning their faces to the light. I told him it had been a coincidence that we drove past; a couple of streets had been closed for resurfacing and I wanted to see whether there were any boys playing football on the church green as in the old days. A pretty house, I said, but the owners were nowhere to be seen. On the other hand, I added, I was surprised when I came across a picture of Atli on page 2 in the paper this morning. He's changed, I said with a laugh, balding and flabby. I couldn't help laughing when I told Anthony about this picture and was forced to put down the receiver when the laughter turned into a coughing fit and I had to reach for a handkerchief while I recovered.

"Is everything all right, Disa?" he asked when I could speak again.

"Everything's fine," I replied.

At two o'clock tomorrow the graduation will take place at the University Cinema. Atli Bollason knows nothing about it, has never known anything. I'm going to wear a blue dress I bought for this trip, as most of my old dresses are now too big for me. This is a well-cut dress which suits me, not least because Anthony came along to advise me when I tried it on.

"What are you going to say to him?" asked Anthony.

I said I didn't know, but hoped I'd think of something over the next few hours.

"Or while I'm sleeping," I said. "Perhaps I'll dream of something sensible for a change."

I miss Anthony but don't let him sense any weakness. I miss him and Old Marshall, the poplar outside my bedroom window and dear Tina whom I was convinced I heard barking while I was still half asleep this morning. I suddenly feel as if she's rubbing herself up against my legs.

"I'm fine," I tell Anthony. "I'm not afraid."

Or so I told Anthony. Yet I'm restless and counting the hours, so I sit down by the window and watch the rays of sunshine falling lazily on to the square, only to stand up again immediately and decide to go down to the restaurant.

I take a seat at a table in the corner, drink tea with lemon and nibble a slice of sponge cake. It's tasteless but it doesn't matter as I have no appetite anyway. Tick, tock, tick, tock. The cathedral clock across the street looks down at me with the arrogance of one who has the upper hand. Tick, tock. Time passes.

His parents have no doubt come to town to attend his graduation. I notice that I write his "parents" without hesitation. This pleases me. I remember how relieved I was when I met them. Remember how kind I found her eyes and the likable diffidence of her husband, that big man. He had just come ashore, putting on his best clothes and running a wet comb through his hair, before they came to fetch him. He stood at a little distance, alternately twining and loosening his fingers. His clothes were tight.

Tick, tock. What can I say to him? After all these years. Do I have anything to say?

I have managed to finish the slice of cake without noticing.

I got back to Reykjavik on the evening of December 30 after a blissfully uneventful journey by seaplane. The mistress came to meet me; I hadn't expected that. She wore a determined expression, a look of resolve which I hadn't been aware of before and her embrace was comforting. It seemed as if my blow had in some way strengthened her.

The Christmas lights were still in place and the scent of pine met us when Maria opened the front door. Dr. Bolli was in his office but came out as soon as he heard us. Ignoring my objections he demanded to be allowed to carry my suitcase upstairs for me. Although it wasn't heavy he still had to put it down and rest twice on the way up. The second time he accidentally grasped a red light bulb in the row of Christmas lights we had wound round the banister intertwined with fir branches. He winced with pain but didn't flinch. I asked him whether I should fetch a cold cloth for his finger but he declined it. I remember his saying: "It'll pass, Asdis. Everything passes."

The son of the house was nowhere to be seen and nobody mentioned him. I would hardly have thought of him if I hadn't caught sight of his galoshes by the basement door. Not finding them very decorative, I shoved them into a cupboard.

On the way up to Fjolugata the mistress had asked me if I'd like to take the next few days off but I told her the truth, that I'd been looking forward to getting back to the kitchen. I explained: "There at least I can convince myself that I'm in charge."

I slept a deep, dreamless sleep that night and woke early on New Year's Eve. There were eighteen to dinner in the evening so there was no time to lose in embarking on the preparations. In the east I could see the first hint of dawn, and the stars were paling, while outside the kitchen window two thrushes hopped along the path, leaving a pale set of tracks. It's a mystery to me why, when I followed their tracks with my eyes, the feeling should suddenly grip me—a virtual conviction—that another world existed which I knew nothing of, not even the shadow. It gripped me for a brief second before releasing me, but held me fast while it lasted. I didn't feel bad afterward but was half distracted at first and didn't come to until I caught sight of myself in my mirror above the stove. That shook me because the expression on my face was unrecognizable. I have never seen it since.

Eighteen to dinner, smoked salmon and duck. There was a good smell in the kitchen by noon when the mistress brought me a glass of port. I wasn't used to alcohol when I cooked but on this occasion it was very welcome.

The rays of the afternoon sun, red-gold and soft, didn't trouble the eyes, though the sun hung low in the sky beyond the trees in the garden, but strayed into the kitchen like curious passersby. The presence of the thrushes was also encouraging, and the calm which comes with the dusk soon arrived. I breathed a sigh of relief. Perhaps I would succeed in directing my thoughts away from my journey north. Perhaps I would find a momentary peace.

Later in the day I heard Atli's voice in the front room. He was talking loudly. I heard his father telling him to go and lie down until dinner.

"Some guests will be coming to see him at midnight," the mistress had told me. "To see in the New Year. The rest of us are going to my brother-in-law's after dinner to play cards."

I ran a bath at five o'clock, changed and did my hair. Then I stood at the window in my room for a while, contemplating the thrushes' tracks in the snow. In the faint glow from the streetlights it was as if they had no beginning and no end.

The mistress invited me to join them in a card game once we'd eaten. I had nothing else to do and felt comfortable with her brother-in-law, Gisli, and his wife, Margret, so I accepted her gratefully. The son of the house remained alone at home, waiting for his guests. His behavior had been strange all evening, though no more than usual. I ignored him, but sometimes found his stare uncomfortable. He had been feeling out of sorts when we sat down at the table but livened up as the evening went on and the whiskey started to take effect. No one could fail to notice that the partying of the last few days had affected him. His father twice quieted him down during the meal, but I was out in the kitchen both times and so didn't hear their exchange of words. The reprimand had the desired effect, though an unreadable smirk remained hovering over his son's lips. It should be pointed out, however, that these exchanges were minor and in no way spoiled the party mood of the dinner guests who showered praise on the food—with sincerity, I must say, rather than from politeness.

It was past ten when we set off to visit Margret and Gisli Haraldsson. I was given a warm welcome and the mistress even called me her foster daughter that evening. She soon took a seat before the piano. There were more people there than I'd anticipated but this didn't bother me. At midnight we drank toasts in champagne and sang "Auld Lang Syne."

"Don't you want to ring Kopasker," asked the mistress, "and wish your father a Happy New Year?"

"The telephone exchange isn't open now," I said.

"Oh, how stupid of me, Disa, how stupid of me."

We women played whist while the men sat in another room with brandy and cigars. There was much laughter. The mistress was in high spirits, calling everyone "darling."

By two o'clock I was tired. I got to my feet and said good night.

"We'll be along shortly," said the mistress.

On the way down to Fjolugata I saw the odd fireworks streaking up into the vault of the sky, only to fizzle away to nothing, but otherwise all was quiet. I entered by the back door, took off my coat and stopped in the kitchen to fetch a glass of milk before bed. There were still guests with the son of the house. The noise carried to me from the drawing room, lower than I'd expected. I recognized Hallur Steinsson's voice immediately, though it was no louder than the others. He was obviously very excited and I moved instinctively closer to the door of the front room in order to listen.

"I'm going to publish the report. No one's going to tell me I can't."

"Do you want to go to prison? How long do you think it would take before the damned British arrested you?"

"What can they do? Who invited them here, may I ask? No, I'll publish Atli's report. Whatever anyone says. Even though the old man has been throwing his weight around."

"Do you want to go to prison too, Atli?"

Silence.

"Atli?"

"Me?"

"Yes, you. Do you want to go to prison, too?"

"You don't even know what I've written."

"Well, read it to us, then."

"Now?"

"Yes, now."

"Hallur . . ."

"Atli, I wouldn't hesitate. You're among friends."

Atli opened the door of the front room. I darted into the kitchen. He went down to the basement, appearing shortly afterward with a sheaf of papers in his hands.

"He even went out to Thingvellir to seek inspiration," said Hallur Steinsson when Atli returned. "I'll publish it. No one's going to tell me that I can't publish it. If it's the last thing I do! The last thing!"

"Read it, Atli."

Four voices. Atli, Hallur, and two others I didn't recognize. I was sure there were only four of them.

"I'm going to read about the trip Bjorn and I took to Dachau."

"Bjorn had the sense to stay in Germany."

"Did I have a choice, Hallur? Did I have a choice?"

"Don't get excited. We know your father forced you to come home. Don't get so excited. Just read it."

He read slowly and clearly. I was surprised that he didn't seem drunk. The others were silent. I moved closer.

"The sun was shining the day we went to Dachau," he began.

Herr Himmler had organized a plane for us from Tempelhof airport and we arrived down south in Bavaria after more than an hour's journey. I've hardly ever seen a man who was as full of energy in all his daily dealings as Herr Himmler. He was always laughing and on excellent terms with everyone. His interest in Iceland was obvious and he spoke very highly of Bjorn's father and the prime minister. He mentioned how impressed he and the Fuehrer were with our history and culture, calling us the only pure, Nordic race left. He is of a very equable temperament and it is his unbreakable rule to treat everyone well . . .

The entrance gate to the prison camp was wide, with a sort of fretwork tower on either side, in my estimation three to four times the height of a man. On top of each tower was a platform fenced in by a grille where two soldiers sat with machine guns and megaphones. Within the fence the prisoners were on the move, apparently all on some sort of errand. Outside the compound were grassy fields and cabbage patches. There were a few sparse clumps of trees and the odd flower bed. In one place there was a pond with ducks on it, containing small fish and minnows . . . Some of the prisoners were from ordinary prisons, transferred to Dachau for their education. There was a shoe factory and weaving room, a carpenter's shop and sewing room. Those who behaved well were permitted to make all kinds of souvenirs for their families and friends . . .

Wherever I went I came across the unique sense of order which characterizes the Germans. To cut a long story short, the prison camp was not unlike a small kingdom, well organized in every way, reflecting in microcosm all the business of life outside. I saw many hideously ugly faces there and admired the tolerance with which the criminals were treated. I mentioned to Commandant Gerlach that some of them looked as if they would hardly turn a hair even if they were roasted on a grid like Saint Laurence. He laughed because he knew what I meant. "What crime have you committed?" I asked one of them. "I murdered my wife," he answered. "And?" prompted Gerlach. "And our four children," the prisoner then admitted. "And my mother, my father and my brother . . ."

Hallur Steinsson burst out laughing. The others joined in.

No one seemed to be particularly badly treated. "It's necessary to do things which may seem unpleasant," I commented to my friend Bjorn, and he agreed. We had spent some time discussing the events of November 9th, *Kristallnacht,* with Herr Himmler as Bjorn is especially interested in the subject. After some thought Bjorn agreed with us that the measures had been unavoidable in the light of the murder of German embassy staff in Paris by the Polish Jew Herschel Grynszpan. He promised to share this information with his father, Ambassador Bjornsson. In connection with this, I pointed out that the first sterilization laws had been Icelandic. Herr Himmler was fascinated when I alluded to the Gragas medieval law code which states: "It is right to castrate vagrants and is not punishable by law, even if they are crippled or die as a result." He asked me to repeat this quotation twice while he made a note of it, he found it so remarkable. He mentioned how the men of old had in many ways been far in advance of us modern men. When Bjorn and I took our leave, he said it meant a lot to him to have our support. He also asked me to remember Foreign Minister von Ribbentrop's message to the Icelandic government, warning them not to be too well disposed toward the British.

"Because we feel friendship for the Icelanders," he said. "We don't want anything bad to happen to you."

I promised that my first job when I got home would be to deliver this message to the government.

We were both proud when we came away from our meeting with him.

"It's important that this should be mentioned," said Hallur Steinsson. "Very important. Go on! Now read about your trip to Buchenwald."

With slow steps I climbed the stairs.

You must have guessed, a voice whispered to me during the night. "We know what's going on," he said to you. "You and I, Asdis."

His hands move up under my blouse and my legs part. A moist tongue on my throat and breasts. Rapid, eager breathing.

Flowerbeds, blue in the evening light. And ducks swimming on the pond. "It's necessary to do things which may seem unpleasant."

He didn't coerce you into anything, he didn't use force, he never threatened you. You lay down, you didn't say: "This is wrong, I don't want to." You didn't walk away. You know you didn't dislike it . . .

Spare me, I say, leave me in peace! Let me hide here in the corner, let me reach out my hand and touch warmth with my fingertips, gentle fingers which lead me away. Lead me away from myself.

I went downstairs at five o'clock. In the drawing room there were still glasses and half-empty bottles of wine on the table. Cigarette smoke lingered in the air. I thought I could hear the echo of his voice in the darkness: "The sun was shining the day we went to Dachau . . ."

In the pale glow from the streetlights I saw a bundle of papers on the dining room table. White papers lying in an untidy heap next to a whiskey bottle. Before I knew it I had them in my hands. Before I knew it I had packed them in my old suitcase along with my clothes and other bits and pieces.

At seven o'clock I walked out into the silent morning of New Year's Day.

I think the waitress was grateful to me for my advice this morning. Admittedly, she seemed rather taken aback at first but soon realized that I was trying to help her.

She must have thought I was English because the couple at the next table had struck up a conversation with me as soon as I sat down. They said they were from Hastings and meant to spend the next ten days traveling around the country. I think they were called Brooks or Bracken or something like that. He said he had been stationed in Iceland during the war.

"Skyr," he said to me, pronouncing the name of the Icelandic yogurt fairly accurately, as if to prove it.

We exchanged commonplaces until the girl came to my table.

"Do you like breakfast?" she asked me.

I gestured to her to come nearer because I didn't want the others to hear.

"I'm Icelandic," I told her, "but if I were English you should say: "Would you like some breakfast, madam?" or "Would you like to see the breakfast menu, madam?"

While we were on the subject, I decided to point out various other things which could be improved. For example, it would be appropriate, I told her, to offer fruit juice, tea or coffee before breakfast itself is served. I also advised her to move more slowly, though I knew she meant well by scurrying from one table to the next.

"You might disturb the guests," I whispered to her.

She seemed to have paid attention and tried to memorize these hints. At least, she wasn't in such a hurry for the remainder of the breakfast sitting and she reacted promptly, bringing me coffee and a glass of orange juice as soon as our conversation was over. Before I got up, I slipped her a note on which I'd written the name of a manual I thought might be of help to her. *Five Hundred Useful Phrases for Waiters and Waitresses,* it's called, compiled by William P. F. Forsythe, the head waiter at the Connaught Hotel in London. Naturally, I wouldn't mention this book to the staff at Ditton Hall, as there we expect polished language and manners to have been part of their upbringing. For foreigners, however, it is very useful.

She blushed slightly when I handed her the note, but thanked me. I told her that later on she should also try to get hold of *Roberts' Guide for Butlers and Household Staff,* though in fact I believed this book was hard to find.

"Don't let the title put you off," I told her, "because there are plenty of things which have remained unchanged even though the book was written in Boston in 1827."

I was pleased to have been able to give this girl some guidance.

A gray wisp of cloud appeared over the hill and was carried swiftly toward me by the cold January blast. I shivered at the window and reached for my sweater on the chair, putting it on over my thin dressing gown. When I looked up, the cloud had dispersed into countless snow buntings, darting in different directions in the sharp gust of wind. A moment later they flocked together again as if their lives depended on it, then vanished from view below the small rise.

The doctor had stepped out of the room.

Grayness all around, gray floor and walls, gray sky, the Christmas lights dimmed. I had been living with Mrs. Olsen for about a week now. She gave me a kinder reception than I deserved when I knocked at her door on New Year's morning. Without asking any questions, she urged me to go and see a doctor when the vomiting had lasted for five days. Through the window I glimpsed the roof of 56 Fjolugata and looked away.

The doctor came in. He smiled.

"Asdis," he said. "I hope congratulations are in order."

In the corridors of the house my memory whispers these

words to me still. On an afternoon stroll when I stop to rest and enjoy the peace and quiet between the cold stone walls, I hear them. "Congratulations. I hope congratulations are in order, Asdis." I jump when a strange voice adds: "You're carrying *his* child. *His* child, Disa."

I remember the doctor hurrying over to me when I sank down. I heard him calling: "Kristin, come here at once! Kristin!"

Two days later I set off to Father at Kopasker.

Months I wish to forget.

The light on my bedside table shone day and night, dim and red, and the wind howled at the windows. When spring came I heard the stream chuckling outside. Nothing disturbed its song but the creak on the stairs when Father came up to see me or the maid brought me something to eat. She had been with us since I was a child, but even so Father made her swear an oath of silence.

"I'll help you," he had said when I arrived. "But you must have the child."

"I can't," I said. "I can't have his child, Father."

He wouldn't be moved.

"I'll see that the child is put in good hands after it's born. But you must have it."

Down in the living room the old clock carried on its futile race against time. I felt it lagged behind with every day that passed and sometimes its chimes passed me by altogether. I had begun to convince myself that the pendulum took a rest in the afternoon but of course this was only my imagination.

Faint, weary chimes. I don't know what's happened to it now.

For the first months I wandered around the house during the day, moving from one chair to another, listening to the silence. Sometimes I sat in the dispensary with Father and watched him preparing medicines or writing reports to send to Reykjavik. In the evenings he often tried to get me to play cards and then we would sit in the dining room with the view of the sea. But I was bothered that time and time again in the twilight I thought I saw a small boat swallowed up by the waves out in the bay. I would get up and go to the window and forget to sit down again. I knew my brain was playing tricks on me but this knowledge did nothing to make me feel better. I thought I could see a lone man in the boat.

At first I would go out in the evenings after darkness had fallen. I rarely walked far and avoided the shore as I was afraid of what might be washed up on land. Instead I sought the moon and stars, rejoicing when I saw the Northern Lights shimmering above the countryside like the wings of the Almighty. It often occurred to me how good it would be to be carried away by them. Disappear. Melt into thin air.

In the end these evening walks became more a source of anxiety than beneficial for my health. Father put pressure on me to take exercise but I was sure the house was being watched.

"Who on earth would do such a thing?" he asked.

I didn't know.

And I'm still none the wiser, as I was a different person during those months. An unknown woman who I hope will never again take up residence in my body. It wasn't I who went out one bright frosty night in April, clad only in a night-dress. Yet I clearly remember the blue moonlight keeping me company over the old riverbed, along the rimed marshes in the direction of the crags. I didn't feel the cold but on the way up the slope where the marshes ended, I was suddenly convinced that I could lean on a moonbeam if I got tired.

The spring beneath the crags was swollen with ice but my childhood refuge was still there between the two friendly tussocks. When I lay down on my back I saw how wondrously close the stars were, like eyes one could trust. Everything will be all right, I thought they were saying, don't worry. Just like when I was a little girl. I closed my eyes and when I opened them next I was lying in my bed with the red glow from the night light flickering around me. I heard the maid calling Father: "She's up! Dr. Jon, she's opened her eyes!"

I didn't get up until two weeks later. Father had looked in on me late that night and seen that I had gone. It saved my life that he guessed where I could be found. Saved mine and my baby's life.

No, it wasn't I who lay unconscious in bed with pneumonia following my near fatal journey out in the freezing cold night, not I who flitted around the house like a ghost that summer, lost track of time, no longer heard the chimes of the clock. Who it was, I don't know, but it wasn't I.

On a bright morning at the beginning of September, when a gentle breeze stirred the curtains, I finally recovered my senses. Perhaps it would be fairer to say that I woke myself, so unprepared was I for the scream. I remember being gripped by panic for a brief moment, as I thought I was listening to Mother's scream when little Bjork was born. For a moment I thought it was her, not me, who lay there in the bed, with Father and the maid leaning over. Yet I was calm. For the first time since my homecoming, I was calm.

I didn't feel any pain, it was more as if the torments which had burdened me for so long were gradually lifting. When he was born it was as if I had been awakened from an enchantment. The clock struck twelve noon. Father laid him wailing in my arms, his heart pumping, and his cry carried out through the open window into the clear autumn air.

It was the most beautiful song ever heard in the country-side.

In the picture my cheek and arm are visible. And Mother's piano can be vaguely glimpsed behind us. He has just finished feeding and is cuddling up to me. I'm looking down into his face.

At first I pleaded with Father not to take this photograph, but gave in at last. He took a long time to prepare the shot, moving more slowly than ever. From his conduct, you might have thought that this ceremony was highly significant.

Once I thought I had lost my photograph. I had woken up in the middle of the night as so often, turned on the light above the bed and opened the drawer in the bedside table to take it out. I usually keep it near me during the day, either between the covers of an old Icelandic cookbook or in my bag if I happen to go out. In the evening I put it back in the drawer of my bedside table before I go to sleep.

That night my fingers encountered nothing. I leaped out of bed and rooted in vain in my bag, before running down to the kitchen, switching on the light and looking first in my old Icelandic cookbook, then in all the other books on the shelves beside the cooker.

My photo was nowhere to be found.

I was in despair by the time I woke Anthony. He was startled for a moment but soon got out of bed to help me. We searched high and low, but it was not until near dawn that I happened to look behind the bedside table and caught sight of it.

Later that day, Anthony and I went down to the village to get copies made. Five copies, all of the same size. I was very anxious until I collected them and repeatedly mentioned to the couple who ran the shop that I trusted nothing would happen to the original. I suspect they took more care than usual as a result.

I brought two copies with me to Iceland, one is in my bag, the other I have propped up against the lamp on the bedside table in my room.

He's cuddling up to me. I'm looking down into his face. Today at two o'clock he's going to graduate.

We were fortunate that the doctor's house was out of the way, a little distance outside the village. Father made sure that no one who wasn't involved would hear of the boy's birth or of the arrangements that were made afterward. Father and his friend, the district magistrate.

That morning I had watched the geese flying in V-formation over the hayfields but now the sky had turned as red as the leaves on the two shrubs by the gate or as the lava gravel on the steps up to the front door. It crunched quietly under their feet when they arrived; I listened to them approaching with slow steps. The maid had made hot chocolate. We drank it in silence; the woman sitting opposite Father and the man standing behind her. Suddenly it grew chilly in the living room and I stood up to close the window. Then I went upstairs.

He was asleep. I had just finished feeding him when they arrived and now he was asleep with the glow of the fading sky on his face. His clothes were ready in a suitcase beside the cradle; I opened it again to make sure that nothing had been forgotten. Afterward, I sat by the cradle and waited for Father to give me the sign.

She smiled instinctively when I brought him down. Her husband took a step nearer, then collected himself and stopped. He bowed his head shyly, alternately twining and loosening his thick fingers. Bowed his head but didn't take his eyes off the boy. I noticed that his clothes were tight on him.

"He," I began, then fell silent. They both looked up. "He likes being stroked on the forehead," I said finally. "Then he calms down," I added. "When he's restless . . ."

I had begun to tremble when I pressed him against me for the last time and breathed in his baby smell. He was still asleep when I handed him over to her.

The lava gravel crunched on the path as they left. In the distance the geese could be heard on their way to their night roost. I stood limply at the living room window, watching them disappear into the dusk.

During the time I spent in Kopasker, Anthony wrote to me no less than once a month. Sometimes I answered him myself but more often I had to ask Father to do it for me. I read the letters over before he sent them and signed most of them. Later, however, I discovered that they had exchanged letters without my knowledge. In these they got straight to the point and were honest about my condition.

Shortly after I came to my senses in May, Anthony began to tell me about Ditton Hall. "I don't know what to do with the family seat," he wrote. "It's standing empty, housing nothing but old memories, some of which are better forgotten. It occurred to me that it might be possible to convert it into a summer hotel. And then I thought of you . . ."

After this he continued in the same vein in every letter.

"My aunt Hilary lived there with her cats when I was a boy. An old harridan with a long, thin nose who was forever scolding. 'Anthony, you mustn't run like that on the stairs! Anthony, you'll frighten the cats!' When she wasn't looking I'd seize the opportunity to squirt water at the beastly creatures, especially in summer when they used to attack the birds. I called her the witch and Mother scolded me."

He and Father had begun plotting behind the scenes.

"I say, Disa. Ditton Hall . . . A country house in a beautiful spot. Who knows, it might do you good to have a change of scene when it's all over . . ."

"All the glass will have to be replaced in the conservatory," wrote Anthony, "but the view is incomparable. In the morning a mist often lies over the fields and then it's pleasant to sit in the conservatory with a hot cup of tea, waiting for the sun to come out. And it's just as nice to sit there at twilight, listening to the birds singing their evening song. Often one will begin and then the rest will join in, their voices dropping as the dusk grows darker. Tweet, tweet. There are no cats any more . . ."

"I say," commented Father. "Such lively birdlife there. That's not bad . . ."

Dear Father, he was so kind. He always warned me when he was expecting a patient. He never blamed me for anything, never showed any displeasure. He was hurt when I told him I didn't want Jorunn to know about my situation but he didn't object. How he contrived it so that my name never appeared on any documents, I've no idea, but of course he risked his reputation. He told the boy's parents (there, I've written "parents" again without a moment's hesitation) that it was up to them whether they chose to tell their son that he was adopted when the time came, but made them promise not to mention me. Only he and I knew the identity of the father.

To prove to me that his ideas about Ditton Hall were not just hollow words, Anthony began to send me advertisements for this and that which he considered it advisable to invest in. Of course, he meant well, though his ignorance was obvious. I've kept these advertisements along with the letters.

The modern Gas Cooker is equipped with every convenience for cooking food scientifically and daintily, said the first advertisement he sent me. The "Zero" Store Cooling and Ice Making Machine was an even more tantalizing phenomenon, *driven by electric motor, steam, gas or oil engines. G. J. Worssam & Son Ltd.* I asked him to wait before purchasing these appliances and the others he'd sent me information about. Especially the Bradford's "Vowel" Washer which he was under the impression was a brand-new gadget. However, those who had come anywhere near household chores at any time during the last quarter of a century knew that this washing machine had long been outmoded.

"There's no question that he's serious, the dear fellow," said Father when he examined the cuttings. "Ice Making Machine, I say . . ."

"I'm so glad you're feeling a bit better," wrote Anthony in late September. "My friends at the Ministry of War Transport have half promised that you can get a passage to England with a cargo ship. They also pointed out that the ship you sailed with to Iceland—the *Bruarfoss*—is still sailing here . . . I know you don't need to be told that the voyage could be risky."

"Risky," read Father, and frowned. "Hm."

When we said good-bye in mid-November, I had the feeling that we would never meet again. I suspect he knew it too. But it still came as a shock when he didn't even survive the war years.

It had started to rain while we were waiting down on the jetty for the boat, first a few drops, then a heavy drizzle turning to fog on the mountains. He was wearing the large, green waxed jacket which he generally wore for visiting patients, and he wrapped it around both of us. The day before he had returned from his third trip to Raufarhofn to check on the boy.

The boat approached, blue, its lights blinking in the fog.

"He's doing well," said Father. "They're taking good care of him. He's a strong, handsome boy."

He remained standing in the same place as we sailed away. I watched him as he was left behind, darkening and growing smaller in the gentle drizzle, until I couldn't distinguish him any longer from the mossy rocks above the shore.

The sound of the telephone wakes me.

I'm startled, but can't hear anything except my own heart-beat and an owl hooting in the distance. The shadow of the poplar quivers on the wall, three branches, two horizontal and one pointing diagonally to the sky. It may be summer, may be winter; Christmas night and my head heavy with food and wine and my mind full of the memories of candle-light and church bells in the village. Or maybe it's spring and a tentative dawn has begun to waken out in the meadow. Maybe it's autumn with steam rising from the damp earth.

The sound of the telephone wakes me without warning as it did fifteen years ago when he was injured. He had been playing down by the jetty and a lorry driver had failed to notice him.

"He's broken his leg," said Dr. Bolli on the phone, "but he's regained consciousness. He's broken a couple of ribs too and has some bruising."

It was autumn and there were raindrops obscuring the window, drawing a gray veil over the brook and Old Marshall's cottage.

"Will he live?"

"He'll live, but the next few months will be difficult."

"I'm coming."

Silence. A long silence.

"They're both with him," he said finally. "His parents."

"His parents." The people who had kept vigil over him when he was ill, seen him take his first steps, taken care of him. Given him a name. Helgi. Helgi Arnason.

My reaction was ludicrous. What did I think I could do? He didn't even know me, didn't know who I was and would no doubt have been frightened of me. Yet I was ready to go. I had to be tough with myself to avoid breaking down. I longed to hold him in my arms, to crush him against me and tell him how much I loved him. But eventually I pulled myself together, my heartbeat slowed and my breathing became regular again.

When the rain stopped, the plants in the garden tubs shook in a chill gust of wind. I moved slowly, the sun came up and the sun went down and the warmth of the embers in the kitchen was comforting.

And so the years passed, each night like an impending punishment, every dream an echo of the telephone ringing in days gone by.

"Tina, dear old lady, sit down here beside me and warm me up." Soon the first rays of sun will stroke the mist from the meadows, gently as a mother caressing her child's cheek.

The phone is silent.

Soon the danger will pass.

The sky suddenly darkened as we were about to take our seats at the table. I had been waiting for him in the lobby. We had no sooner greeted each other than it began to rain; we hadn't even released each other's hands, though we had begun to take the first steps in the direction of the dining room. We stopped automatically to watch the rain drumming on the road and on the lawns around the independence hero's statue on the other side of the street, until old Bolli, my former employer, looked at his watch and said: "I hope it'll clear up before the graduation ceremony begins."

He's aged, poor dear. After all, he's nearly eighty, and moves slowly, though he's not exactly unsteady. His hearing's going, he says, but his voice is as quiet as ever.

"I hope it won't last," he repeats as we sit down. "It was such beautiful weather this morning."

I remember the day I last saw him. It was the morning I sailed for England, November 18, 1941.

I had rung his office two days earlier to announce my arrival. I could hear in his voice that the last thing he'd expected was a call from me but nevertheless he agreed without hesitation that our conversation should be confidential. He welcomed me, his handshake as limp as now, his eyes as distant as ever. (Now there seem to be cataracts over them as if they are gradually being extinguished or even turning inward.) His secretary brought us coffee and we sat in deep leather chairs by the window. I glanced at a painting of him and two other men with graying hair, above the desk. He noticed and, half sheepish, said by way of explanation: "A present from the staff when I was fifty."

A thick Persian rug on the floor, timber paneling on the walls, bookshelves by the door, silence. On the desk were a few papers under a silver-plate paperweight, while beside them perched a glaring stuffed falcon. On the table between us lay a few pebbles; he picked one of them up and turned it absentmindedly between the thumb and index finger of his left hand. I glanced outside. In the window there were eight panes, the lower ones were opaque but the upper ones admitted the light without hindrance. The cloudless sky was visible above the rooftops across the street.

When I explained my business and asked him to promise life-long discretion, he nodded after a moment's thought. I had half expected him to try to evade my request with a smile or a few well-meaning words but perhaps he didn't get the chance.

He nodded and sat without speaking while I told him about my relationship with his son Atli, the reading on New Year's Eve (I didn't mention that I'd snatched the papers before leaving 56 Fjolugata), the months at Kopasker, my little boy, and the fisherman and his wife from Raufarhofn who had adopted him.

He sat in silence, and stopped turning the pebble over between his fingers, stroking it instead with his thumb as if it were fragile.

288

"No one except my father knows who the father is," I said. "You don't need to keep an eye on the boy except from a distance."

The sun shone through the window on his pale cheek. He screwed up his eyes and moved out of the glare.

"Why are you confiding in me?" he asked finally.

"My father is getting on," I said. "And Arni is a fisherman . . ."

"I'm sorry?"

"His father," I explained.

"Oh, yes. His father, yes."

"And who knows what will become of me. Better safe than sorry."

The coffee was cold; perhaps it hadn't been sufficiently hot when his secretary brought it.

"So you're sailing today."

"This evening."

"Sea air is supposed to be good for the health. I wish you bon voyage, Asdis."

I had no choice but to trust him. Watching him now as he reaches for the sugar bowl and puts a white sugar lump into his mouth, I remember how I grew calm in his presence.

"I do hope it'll clear up in good time," he says. "It was such fine weather this morning."

The waitress, whom I had advised to improve her English, seems a bit nervous as she approaches our table. I smile at her.

"I even miss the days when she was at her worst," he says, breaking the silence. "You know she was fond of you."

I'm not prepared for this and have to clear my throat before I can reply.

"It was mutual," I say. "I often think of her."

The rain drums on the road outside. We eat slowly. I'm not hungry but the food is edible. The girl doesn't seem afraid of me any more.

"Five Hundred Useful Phrases for Waiters and Waitresses," I say to her when she removes our plates.

"William Forsythe," she says archly.

"William P. F. Forsythe," I add.

We stand up.

"Are you nervous at all?" he asks.

We set off hand in hand.

"I think I've made up my mind what to do," I reply.

"Good. Good. That makes me feel better."

Flickering silhouettes, a faint echo.

Lights ahead of me, a far-off glimmer, noise, roars of laughter. My former employer leans over to me and whispers something in my ear but I can't catch the words. Through the open side entrance I can see sunshine on the damp lawn. I listen as I think I can hear a bird chirping incessantly now that the rain has stopped. It reminds me of the blackbird in my poplar early in the morning when the blue-gray light creeps across the fields and feels its way down the branches of the trees. I listen but then the old man leans over to me again.

"He's a swimming champion," he whispers. "Have I already told you that?"

He's sitting between his parents diagonally opposite us. I saw them enter and bowed my head involuntarily, even though I'm sure they wouldn't recognize me. Since they sat down I've been staring at him but have sometimes had to look away.

"Ladies and gentlemen. I would like to welcome you . . ."

The side entrance closes and the songbird is silenced. Before I go down in the morning and light the fire, Tina and I generally sit by the window watching the blackbird through the glass. She scratches politely at the door to let me know she's there, and rubs up against me as soon as I let her in. We wait for the light to reach along the branches of the poplar and touch the wings of the blackbird. When it flies with the light up into the quiet morning air we stand up and go downstairs. And I say, "Daylight has come, Tina. A new day."

I have to look away.

"He's very like you, Asdis," says the old man.

They come in hand in hand, he and his mother, his father walking a few paces behind, as bowed and as shy as ever. He stops all of a sudden as if he has got lost and come to an unknown turning, before continuing. When they sit down he runs a comb through his gray hair.

He smiles easily, my son. Tall, fair-complexioned and smiling. I see when he leans over to his father that he knows he's ill at ease in this company. I see how fond he is of him.

"Ladies and gentlemen. No one knows what the future will bring but with this education under your belt . . ."

People rise, we move down to the lobby. The sky is still cloudless but I forget to listen for the songbird. A cloudless sky; the puddles on the pavement outside evaporating.

I see them come out of the hall behind us. His parents vanish into the crowd while he joins a group of his friends by the cloakroom. Dr. Bolli and I walk out and hail a taxi. The old man climbs in. I'm about to get in beside him, then ask him to wait for me for a moment.

"I have to see him once more," I say. "Just once."

I walk back in and squeeze through the crowd, half blinded after the sunshine. A tremor runs through me and I have to lean against the wall while I recover. He's still in the same place with his schoolmates by the cloakroom. I approach, then stop. He's happy. I can tell he's happy. I stand motionless, watching him, and when he turns his back to me I walk further into the lobby so that I can see his face. My progress through the crowd is slow and just as I'm passing the cloak-room he turns round and walks straight into me. I jump and drop my bag on the floor. It opens and a couple of things spill out of it: my lipstick and the photo of him in my arms.

"Sorry," he says. "I'm terribly sorry."

He bends down first to pick up my bag and lipstick, then reaches for the picture. When he hands it to me, I take his hand. For a split second I hold his hand. He smiles.

"Thank you," I say.

We drive away bathed in sunshine. I sit in silence because I don't want to lose the sound of his voice. When I close my eyes I fix his face in my memory. He's smiling.

I'm calmer. I've found him. From now on he'll always be with me.

During the last few days I've been wondering whether the squirrels in the garden can sense a hard winter ahead.

I've been sitting in the conservatory and wondering, as they've been busy lately hoarding nuts and scampering away to hide them, two in particular, one of them a bit lame. I mentioned the squirrels to Anthony, and the crows which perch almost daily on a post down by the brook, hunched over their own shadows. He merely seemed surprised that I should already be thinking about the winter.

It's still warm and sunny most days, showers are few and mild and the sunshine is merry in the green foliage. There is no sign of the heralds of autumn except perhaps in the early morning breeze or the song of the grasshopper at twilight. And yet my thoughts have turned to the winter and I've mentioned to Old Marshall that it might be best to prepare for it earlier rather than later this year.

This afternoon his daughter Lydia is coming round with her son. We've arranged that she should leave him with me for a few hours because he wants to have a game of cards and play with the train set I bought last year. He spoke to me on the phone yesterday and asked whether I would bake him waffles with cream and syrup. "I like them so much, Miss Disa," he said. I'm so looking forward to seeing him.

Yesterday I received a letter from little Marilyn, which I didn't deserve as I haven't got round to replying to the one she wrote me while I was in Iceland. Anyway, it was nice to get her letter and I read it with pleasure on my way home from visiting Dr. Ellis and again when I woke up this morning. The envelope also contained a photograph of the two of us, taken when I visited her this summer en route to Leith. A lovely picture which I'm going to find a good spot for in the kitchen, probably on the shelf under my mirror. She's smiling in the photograph and as I examine it better and read her letter more carefully, I get the distinct impression that our conversation that evening has done her some good.

For the last few days a wisp of cloud has hung in the top branches of the trees which encircle the fields. Today it's glowing and in the evenings it catches the pale gleam of the moon. Sometimes I convince myself it's a message to me, a tuft of wool caught on the Almighty's barbed-wire fence. There it is for the fifth day in a row and I'm getting used to it. Old Marshall, on the other hand, distrusts it; I saw him standing outside his cottage for a long time yesterday, contemplating it.

During the day I carry on jotting down this and that to pass the time and cheer myself up. I have enough leisure for this, since I hardly go near the cooking anymore as my strength is failing. But I don't feel unwell and I enjoy listening to the echoes from the tennis courts in the afternoon lull—dunk, dunk—like a clock that's running down. I wait for Anthony to walk across the lawn when the game is over and drink a glass of lemonade with me. I told him yesterday that I trusted the girl absolutely to take over from me. "The girl," I say, but ought to mention that she's about thirty. We appointed her at the beginning of the summer at the instigation of a friend of mine in Lyon, once I saw that her attitude to cookery was the same as mine. She's extremely able and, I must say, has even improved since she came here. I appreciate that Anthony's begun to bear up better when the conversation turns to the future.

It's still light but I go to bed early these days. When I close my eyes my son is always with me. His voice sounds in my ears, comforting me, and my hands are warmed by the touch of his palm. He's with me, his complexion as bright as a spring morning. It wasn't all for nothing, then, I tell myself. You did do something good.

At night I often dream the same dream. I'm standing out in the garden in bright moonlight. Tina is with me. On the other side of the brook there are two horses looking over at me. I think I can see the whites of their eyes. There's frost on the grass but I'm not cold when I set off. I haven't walked far when I realize I'm resting both hands on a slender moonbeam. This always takes me by surprise, and falling instinctively to my knees I draw a little songbird in the frost with the moonbeam.

When I awake, I have the feeling that it will burst into song with the coming of spring.